Toy Soldiers

1: Apocalypse

by

Devon C Ford

D1736284

Dedicated to everyone who puts on their brave face every day and always tells you that they are fine.

Stay Strong.

COPYRIGHT

Cover design by Claire Wood at:

www.spurwingcreative.co.uk

Prologue

They say the eyes are the window to the soul.

Given that the damn things clearly didn't have souls, then their eyes made a little more sense. As he looked into a pair of the milky, shrouded orbs from a distance he was very uncomfortable with, he could see nothing behind them.

That wasn't entirely true; he could see that the eyes used to be a light brown, maybe even hazel, but the thing, that *something* which made a person an actual living person, just wasn't there. Drawing back from the crack in the door, tentatively held by a weak chain fastened into the wood that used to give people a ridiculously false sense of security, he raised his trusted corpse-sticker and eased one of the tines of the old pitchfork through the milky eyeball with an unpleasant squelch, feeling little resistance until the tip of the metal probed far enough into the brain to disrupt whatever happened in there.

The thing that used to have light brown eyes stopped moaning, stiffened, then exhaled slowly and slumped, like its batteries had run out in fast-forward. The gap it left was filled rapidly by another one, and his heart began to pump a little too hard in response to the ear-splitting screech that ripped from its mouth. The biggest problem with getting caught up in fighting them instead of avoiding them was focus.

By that, he meant that a person can easily get so focused on the hissing, moaning, screaming things, on the dead teeth snapping and moaning and the broken fingers reaching for them, that their concentration wouldn't let in any other information that they needed. Having been caught out more than once over the last months, and only surviving by dumb luck, he liked to think he was starting to tune in to that.

Luckily for him because, as soon as he'd stuck another one in its squishy brain, like you'd be tempted to with a facia salesman who had overstayed his welcome at the front door, the stumbling, moaning sounds began to come from behind him. From inside the house. He stuck a third, somehow gauging that he had time before the moaning behind him became his next priority, before turning to regard the next horror he had to face.

Now the smell wasn't anywhere near as bad as the first few weeks, especially if they'd been trapped inside where the rain couldn't freshen up their stale flesh, but the thing that descended the stairs still possessed an aura that made his eyes sting. It was a musty, dried-out aroma that was almost sickly. That sickly-sweet smell catapulted him back to memories he'd intentionally forgotten, which now fought with all the other things going on in his head for space at the front of the queue.

The memories, encouraged by a random smell as they so often were, threatened to momentarily debilitate him; to send him back into the mind of the naive nine-year-old child he had been when it had all started, and make him want to rush past the thing coming down the stairs at him, so that he could hide under his bed.

Only this isn't my house, he thought, *the thing coming down the stairs isn't my alcoholic mother, reeling from another all-day session. And hiding under a bed here is as sensible as shooting myself in the head.*

Less sensible, actually.

An unbidden and natural change in footing to line up square to his nearest threat, a controlled thrust forward, followed by the equally brisk withdrawal of the weapon, then a short wave of satisfaction as the thing dropped lifelessly to the musty carpet to remain still.

Not looking back, he used his meagre body weight to shut the partially open and tenuously secured front door. One of the benefits of fighting things that have been in that weirdly suspended state, in most cases for many months, was that they were physically pretty soft. That general softness rewarded his actions with a soft patter as three digits, severed by the closing of the door, tumbled lightly onto the carpet where they twitched once each, then went still.

Shuddering, he thanked whatever thing up there looked out for people that they weren't the rare kind of fresh ones, and returned his attention to getting out of the house without having to fight his way through the nest he'd just disturbed in the innocent-looking bungalow opposite. He hefted his weapon of choice ahead of him ready for any more crusty ones still hidden and dormant within. Dormant, that was, until some idiot burst through their front door to get away from the dozen or so other things outside.

Finding that the downstairs of the house was empty, he decided to get the hell away from it without raiding the cupboards, before the crowd out the front flowed around the sides like water and cut off any chance of escape.

Minutes later, jogging uncomfortably with the sole of one shoe flapping noisily with each awkward step, he thanked that same unknown deity for his managing to escape another bloody situation that should have killed him.

I guess I was just lucky, he told himself. But to know just how lucky, he supposed he should start from the beginning.

Chapter 1

1989

Living on a farm in what was basically the arse-end of nowhere had its perks for a boy of nine. His older sister said she felt trapped there, but he thought it was the ultimate freedom.

A few years after moving there, he thought he'd learned enough about life to know that her feelings of being trapped were nothing to do with the geography.

There were some surrounding villages, and a dozen or so other places in sight if you climbed on top of the biggest barn, but other than that it was totally isolated. He thought the farm was the biggest single place on earth, but then again, he was young when his family moved there.

He'd been in that happy bubble of childhood ignorance for years, right up until he noticed that things had begun to change at home. He and his sister had to walk just under two miles to the main road where their bus would take them towards the bigger towns along the south coast, and their schools were on an army base. This was another happy note from way back when in his mind; stopping lessons and being allowed to run to the window to watch a convoy of Chieftain tanks roll by with an impossibly loud roar caused by their heavy tracks.

Hundreds of tonnes of armour screeching past on their way to the training grounds, feeding the fantasies of the children.

Some of the other boys bragged about how they bet their Dad was in one of them, or about how their Mum did something else equally heroic. He remembered one particular time that happened, when he retook his seat with a sudden shroud of realism, of unhappiness, and he finally saw the difference between him and the other kids.

His Dad wasn't driving a tank. If he was driving anything it was a tractor on the farm, and his mother didn't work because she... well, he didn't know why; all he did know was that if she didn't get her glass bottles with her special water in that he wasn't allowed to touch, and if she ran out of her cigarettes, then all hell would break loose in the house. With that cloud of realism descending permanently on him and never leaving, he suffered the taunting of other children as he cried in the middle of the classroom.

The truth was, he had been shielded from a lot of the bad things that went on under 'the roof that had been provided for him', a refrain he had heard shouted so often; like a roof made anything better. His sister was the one, he realised much too late, who had protected him. It was she who threw herself in front of their parents to take the punishment he had apparently earned, and she did it tight-lipped, so she couldn't cry out and give either of them the satisfaction of knowing they had caused someone pain.

That only made things worse, and by the time he knew something was truly wrong and his behaviour invited more punishments, she had already hurt herself once too often to cope with the pressure.

To that day, despite every unfathomable, insane thing that had since transpired, he could still see the vivid images of his sister being taken away to hospital, screaming his name, telling him to be brave as she kept fighting all the way until the van doors slammed shut to muffle her voice.

"Good bloody riddance," his – *their* – mother spat at the white ambulance as it shrank into the distance, until finally rounding a bend and being swallowed up into the green surroundings. "Ungrateful little cow never knew which side her bread was buttered."

With that last cruel and callous remark, she lit another cigarette and scowled down at her son, smacking him hard across the back of his head. He looked back up at her and was careful to keep the rebellion out of his eyes. He could tell that she was desperate to say something, almost itching to respond to the words she expected from him, so he stayed silent.

"That was for nothing," she said smugly as she turned away, "and there's plenty more where that came from, you little shit."

He still said nothing, just watched her back and imagined the actions before her: transfer cigarette to right hand, pick up bottle and unscrew cap with left hand, pour, put down bottle, drink, inhale on cigarette.

His father's presence suddenly stabbed his consciousness and his gaze darted to him. He had let the edge of the curtain fall by then, having watched the ambulance drive out of sight, just as the young boy had, Then the father turned from the window to face him. He couldn't tell whether his father was angry with him or not, but his face was heavy with blame.

"Go to bed," he growled at the boy.

"But I haven't had any tea…" he said reflexively, regretting his outburst instantly.

Crossing the room in two long strides, his father's hand followed suit and struck him just where his mother had, rocking him off his feet this time. Pausing a moment on his knees to fight the tears back inside his eyes, he stood and climbed the stairs to go to bed hungry. Before he had even closed his bedroom door fully, he heard the nightly argument downstairs begin with real venom.

That night was when his childhood ended, in the late spring of 1989, but that happened to coincide with the end of the whole damned world.

The following morning, he was awake early, having spent what felt like all night trying to hold back more tears caused by his aching belly.

He had dressed for school after darting a hand out from under the warm covers to retrieve the uniform, which had been washed, dried and ironed by his sister. He'd placed it ready the night before, and wriggled into it without getting out of bed.

One of the unwelcome delights of living so remotely was that the place was permanently cold, unless in the summer when it was unbearably hot for a few weeks. He hated the cold and couldn't face the prospect of getting out of a warm bed into the chilly air to strip off and get into cold garments. His system was, to him at the naïve age of nine, a stroke of pure genius.

Having stayed under the covers until the new clothes were warm, he climbed out and carefully made his bed so as not to offer any opportunity to earn a punishment. He gently kissed the soft stuffed toy lamb which had been his sister's, hid him gently under the pillow, and went downstairs.

His mother normally didn't surface until after he had to leave for school, but that morning he found them both up and staring at the television set. Like all young boys his age, he was obsessed with the new colour television in the lounge. There was talk of there being a fifth channel soon, and he just hoped that there would be some programmes he would be allowed to watch.

Seeing both of his parents still and inexplicably silent, he helped himself to a piece of toast from a chipped plate and leaned around their legs to see what was so interesting.

"…have confirmed reports of violent behaviour and cannibalism in those affected by the mysterious disease. Our correspondent in London has more…" said the woman sitting behind her desk on the screen.

The picture changed to shaky filming of something he couldn't make out, like a riot, and his need for information blinded him to the risks of speaking aloud.

"What's going on?" he asked, feeling the air rip in two with the simultaneous scream and yell of fright that tore from them both. Fearing instant physical reprisal, he threw myself clear and, sure enough, a meaty hand whistled though the air to miss him by an uncomfortable margin. Evidently deciding that he was too far away to be worth the effort of leaving the television screen, his mother satisfied herself by flicking the ash of her cigarette towards him with an accompanying vicious glare.

"Go to school, now," she shrieked and turned away to reach towards the set to twist the volume dial up high.

Retreating to the kitchen, he looked around for his lunchbox, finding it still bearing the mouldy crusts and wrappers from the last time. His heart dropped with the reminder that his sister wasn't there to look out for him anymore, and it both saddened him and strengthened his resolve.

Snatching up more toast before he could be noticed again, he opened a kitchen cupboard to grab crisps and the last chocolate biscuit, all crunchy goodness nestled inside its foil and paper wrappers.

Then he pulled open the unlocked front door to put his shoes on in the porch. Still being ignored, not that him telling them he was half an hour early would make a difference, the young boy left his parents to their TV and snatched up his parka to head up the lane as he ate the toast.

After half a mile, and having passed all of the farm buildings to his right and open fields to his left, he walked past the three small houses nestled in a side road and surrounded by tall pines. They were called The Pines, ingeniously. Normally there would be some activity there, but today there was nothing. Ignoring the sense of unease he felt, he trudged onwards to pass the only other entrance off the lane before it met the main road. That track always seemed dark and foreboding to him, and together with his sister, he had made up stories about the dark deeds which had occurred there.

Legend had it, or at least the legends they had conjured, that an old woman lived there. Alone in her mansion, she protected the money she had inherited against anyone who came to steal it. That inheritance had cost her family dearly, as she had killed everyone who was ahead of her until it was all hers.

They had laughed about her, not that either of them had ever seen her or even knew if she truly existed, and they took turns in scaring one another when they passed by the overgrown entrance twice a day.

Eventually reaching the wider road, which to his child's eyes seemed like a motorway because there were white lines painted on the pitted surface, he settled down with his backside on the top bar of a wooden gate to keep the rest of him out of the dewy-wet grass. The toast had long been finished and he considered tucking into the two items which constituted his entire lunch, but disciplined himself to hold out.

It wasn't as though he could beg food from his friends at school at lunch time; with his sister gone he had nobody to speak to now anyway.

As that harsh reality finally convinced his brain of the recent facts and what they meant, his tears flowed to fill the time until the tired coach pulled up to hiss its creaking door open.

Chapter 2

The long coach ride was uncomfortable, as he'd already passed two boys who he knew would pick on him as soon as they were kicked out into the warzone of the playground. Not having his sister to talk to and keep the others away, he knew he would be in for some trouble even before the first bell sounded.

The seats were usually half-filled by the time they climbed on board, but that day there seemed to be fewer children there. He considered this as he stared out of the vibrating window, looking through the shroud of condensation and over rolling fields passing by at speed outside.

All he saw were flashes, glimpses, of the world beyond his control. Sheep in one hilly patch of fenced hillside. Black and white cows in another, a flatter enclosure, a small stream that blinked by, replaced by a pub with a slide and swings in the garden beside it. His journey passed by like this, in reflective loneliness, as he dreaded arriving at school to spend an uncomfortable day in the relative safety of being away from the reach of his parents. As the coach hissed to a jerking stop, he sighed in tired resignation and gathered himself to endure what came next. Stepping down and keeping his eyes on the ground, he made straight for the cover of a massive tree near the entrance, where he just hoped he could avoid any interaction.

Kicking his feet in the soft, brown pine needles which had fallen from the high branches, he waited for the bell, but he also waited for what came whenever his sister wasn't with him.

"Oi, Pee Wee," came the voice of the boy who had been his tormentor since his first day in school, "where's your mummy?" he taunted, meaning his sister. That was one of the vagaries of rural life; schools combined on single sites with some classes only holding a handful of kids. Often, school years even combined if there weren't enough children of the right age, and that varied greatly due to the fact that half of the kids there were from the military base nearby. Whenever vast numbers shipped out, their kids would often move with them and affect the number of empty seats in the school.

The boy who approached him now, yelling out in his high-pitched voice the cruel nickname he had branded him with years before, was called Edward.

And Peter hated him.

He looked up, unwittingly making eye contact with the small, sunken dull eyes buried in the fat, rosy cheeks of the bully walking his way. As always, Edward was flanked by two more boys who enjoyed the humiliation of others. After all, where was the fun in bullying someone without an audience?

"I said where's your mummy, Pee Wee?" he said again, too loud to be just for his victim's benefit and obviously planning a display.

"Not coming," Peter muttered, eyes glued to his shoes as they shuffled uncertainly in the soft, pine-covered dirt.

"Speak up," Edward barked, emulating the military bearing he saw in others but possessed none of himself. Edward's father was another farmer, but pigs instead of dairy like the milk farm he lived on. Everything about the boy seemed to get Edward's back up, and not a day at school had ever gone by without him hurting him in some way.

"She's not coming," Peter said slightly louder as he began walking away. Coming out of the warm cover of the tree's shelter he felt the light rain sting his face just as the sound of footsteps echoed behind him. Edward was chasing him down, his followers easily matching pace with the overweight, pugnacious bully.

"Oi," he snarled, "where are you going? I haven't finished talking to you yet?"

Something in the way he spoke reminded Peter of his parents, of the cruelty of having someone in your power and forcing them to endure the expectation of pain before it came. He stopped and turned, seeing the evil glee in his fat face before he lined up to hit him.

He didn't know if it was the hunger he felt making him angry. He didn't know if it was the pain of loneliness and seeing his sister taken away, whether it was the air of tingling fear that something bigger was wrong, or whether he had just been pushed too far by a combination of these things.

Acting on instinct, he kicked out, hitting the fat boy in his shin and dropping him to roll around the concrete wailing in high-pitched agony. His followers stopped, both looking at the boy in shock. Neither of them made a move to do anything, not even to protect their fearless leader and certainly not to step into his place.

Peter stood rooted to the spot, holding his ground and wearing a teary-eyed look of determined rage as Edward cried at his feet. The others glanced behind him and backed away, melting into obscurity expertly just as Edward had sat up and rolled his trouser leg up to expose a graze and bruising which was already beginning to spread.

"What's going on here?" said a stern voice from above their heads. The teacher who had seen the altercation, or at least had his attention drawn by the end of it, took one look at the scene he was presented with and grabbed the neck of Peter's coat roughly. Finding himself hauled round and forced to run on tiptoes to keep pace and not strangle himself, he was whisked away from the danger of instant reprisal towards the school office.

"Peter," said the voice above him as he was thrust through the wooden doors, "I'm very disappointed in you."

Me? He thought, *why do I get the blame for that?*

Those thoughts stayed in Peter's head, because he had learned long ago never to argue or the punishments were doubled.

He sat in a chair as he was told, eyes fixed on the floor past his dangling shoes which caught the occasional tear falling from his eyes, and he waited for the punishment. He didn't have to wait long, as he was called in to the headmaster's office.

"I don't have time to deal with this today," he started before Peter had even closed the door behind him. "You will be punished for that," he went on distractedly pointing a finger at the wall which eventually led towards the playground and the scene of the crime, "and I will write to your parents. With that said," he went on in a more careful tone, "I am also informed of the circumstances surrounding your sister. So today, instead of having lunch, you will write a letter of apology to Edward."

The indignation of unfairness combined with the knowledge of her fate stung Peter into looking up, a fire burning inside him that made him want to rage against the teachers and the bully, but he managed to suppress that just in time before he earned more punishment.

"As I have said," the teacher went on in a lower voice as his eyes darted over papers on the expansive desk, "I have more important things to deal with today, so you can leave now; be back here at lunchtime."

Peter stood, taking his dismissal stoically, and walked out of the office to the blessed sound of the bell ringing. He shuffled his way towards his class, climbing the single flight of stairs to the first floor of the huge, square building.

Something seemed off; just as the bus had been less populated than usual, so was the school almost half-empty. Pushing through the door into the classroom, he saw too many empty chairs, and the buzz of chatter was higher than normal. He feared the consequences of that noise, evidently alone in that fear as everyone else was talking loudly. Edward hobbled in, emphasising the ridiculous limp he had employed for sympathy, and fixed Peter with a glare that spoke of copious amounts of painful revenge. Pushing that unwelcome thought away, he glanced around at the half-filled desks and was struck by a realisation.

Not one child from the army base was there.

Not sure what that meant, he sat in silence and waited for the teacher. After five minutes, according to the large wall clock that usually ticked noisily but couldn't be heard over the din now, they were still without a teacher. That had never happened before, and almost as though the collective children grew bolder by their lack of overlord, the noise rose once more. Just as anarchy threatened to overcome the group, the door burst open and the headmaster stood in the threshold. He looked drawn and stressed, and he declared loudly that all pupils must attend the assembly hall.

As with all creatures of habit, they lined up by the door as a class in register order, like they always had done. The thought that nobody was enforcing the rules never even occurred to any of them.

As one, they traipsed back down the stairs in a slow-moving caterpillar-like approximation of their inward journey, then waited as they filed in to sit cross-legged on the polished parquet floor. The noise subsided as the headmaster stood in the centre of the stage and called once for hush. He spoke only once, then followed his instruction with a glowering look which he fixed on the younger children in the front row. That look silenced them as quickly as his words had, and the silence spread like a disease that rapidly infected the entire room.

Risking a glance around, Peter saw that the back half of the hall was empty when it would normally be full, and that half of the teachers who hovered at tactical points along the outer walls to watch for unruly behaviour were also not there.

"I have an announcement," the headmaster said loudly, before a screeching, rumbling sound ripped the air as it grew in intensity. The children were all accustomed to the sounds of heavy tanks moving, but this convoy seemed bigger, louder and longer than any they had ever heard before. The seconds stretched into minutes, until finally the roaring din of heavy metal began to subside and fade into the distance.

"I have an announcement," the head master intoned again finally, holding up a piece of paper and restoring his reading glasses to the end of his nose with his right hand.

"School will be closed from now until further notice. All children are to go home until the school instructs them to return."

The hall erupted into talk, answered by the raised voices and shouts of teachers trying to restore order, which was achieved shortly afterwards. One class at a time they were shepherded out and back to their classes to await their collection from the chilly playground.

After what seemed like an impossibly long time spent avoiding Edward and his accomplices whilst maintaining a watchful eye on his whereabouts, the coach returned with a very confused and annoyed looking driver at the wheel. Grateful for the relative safety from persecution, Peter returned to stare out of the same steamed-up windows on the return leg of his daily journey.

Unsurprisingly, he found nobody waiting for him at the end of the road. Occasionally, if the mood took either of them or when there was a false sense of affection towards him and his sister, one of them would bring a vehicle to the end of the road and sit smoking until the coach dropped them off on the far side of the fast stretch. Had there been more traffic, his sister had told him, then the road would be very dangerous. As it was, only sporadic cars passed that way even if they did drive fast, and they could be easily avoided.

With a sigh, he looked both ways twice, listened carefully for the sound of any approaching engines, just as his sister had taught him, and carefully stepped across the road to the grass-covered central reservation.

Repeating the process for the second road that bore cars coming from his left this time, he crossed again and began the trudge home.

Peter hoped that school had telephoned his parents, otherwise he would be accused of missing the bus and lying to get a day off school. Quite why they ever thought he would choose their company over the bullies and the teachers, Peter could never understand.

Opening his lunchbox on the move, he took out the only food he'd had chance to steal and ate it before he returned home and ran the risk of losing it.

Chapter 3

Finally rounding the last bend in the road, the one where his sister had disappeared around, going the other way in the ambulance, Peter came in sight of the farm buildings and the house he called home. Getting to the front door, he put his hand on the handle to turn it, finding it uncharacteristically unyielding.

The doors are never locked, he told himself, trying to fathom why today he couldn't get back in. His sister would know what to do, but that thought was as useless as the tears he had shed already. Rolling back the heavy cabinet which held boots and a film of dust and dried mud, Peter found the small leather key fob which was attached to the spare. He wasn't supposed to know about it, but it had been there for years since his mother had once left her keys in the pub before getting a lift home.

It wasn't that she was being responsible by not driving their car back, but more that she was so drunk that she didn't remember driving there, and so abandoned the car by accident. Instead of addressing the larger problem, she had made sure she had a spare in case his father chose not to let her in like he did that time. Having long given up on drinking in public, she had spent the last year drinking cheaper spirits at home, where nobody dared judge her or pass comment on her, bypassing the glass entirely some nights.

Sliding the key into the lock, Peter hesitated before opening it in case it attracted punishment.

Leaving the door locked, he replaced the key and the cabinet carefully, then walked a lap around the house to look for something, anything, to explain the strange day's occurrences.

The car wasn't on the driveway; not entirely uncommon but less common nowadays since the drinking began at breakfast and carried on through. The dog wasn't in the house, otherwise she would be barking at his return, but that too wasn't uncommon as Peter's father would likely have her at his heel on the farm somewhere. Sitting on the step in the overgrown back garden, Peter tried to think of the best thing to do that wouldn't get him in trouble.

Going onto the farm, especially in his school uniform, which was on its first day out of the five that it had to last, was a bad idea. His father would rage at him if he found him playing there when the daily movements were going on. The beating he had taken when he tried to follow him to work one day last summer was still fresh in his mind. He had come face to face that day with a young bull which was being herded in his direction. Peter shuddered at the memory and the feeling of fear; not from the animal who had just demonstrated an alarming aggression, but from his father, who had promised worse injuries than the bull could inflict if he ever disobeyed him again.

He didn't know how long he waited, but it was long enough for the slight chill of the morning to creep into his body.

Getting up and going into the large shed that was called the workshop, he turned on the electrical breaker to make the power flow to the simple building covered by its wriggly-asbestos panelled roof. Hearing the radio burst into low static as soon as it woke with the fresh feed of power, he stepped towards it and began to turn the dial gently to try and find some music. The fine-tuning of a radio was a skill he had learned but not yet perfected, so when he first heard the voices speaking intently with an edge of stress, Peter struggled to find it again after reversing the direction of the dial too far. Eventually, painstakingly turning it a fraction each time, he found the voices once more.

"…unconfirmed reports coming from the capital throughout the night, but it is certain that the military has been deployed on the streets of London. Looting and riots have erupted, but eye-witness accounts have stated that the infected are at the heart of the troubles. A spokesperson from the London Metropolitan Police Force has urged all residents of the city and surrounding areas to stay in their homes and not to infringe on the activities of the emergency services." A pause sounded, punctuated only by Peter's eyebrows meeting in the middle, until the newsreader started again.

"In other news, after their two-nil victory over Albania last month, the England football team have announced that they are confident of another win ahead of the return leg when Albania travel to Britain next month in the world cup qualification rounds…"

His attention faded away from the sports news, finding it perverse that people could be so casual as to talk about a football match when, to him at least, it sounded like London was burning to the ground. The sound of a loud engine outside brought him back to reality, making him quickly run from the shed to flick off the electricity breaker on his way out. He stopped running as he rounded the edge of the house to see his parents sitting in the front seats of the car, both smoking and arguing intently, with hands waving to make their points. They hadn't seen their son yet, and he preferred it that way, so he kept still with just a part of his face showing around the edge of the brick.

Peter's mother evidently said something his father didn't like, because he started hitting the steering wheel with enough force to rock the car on its springs and crush the cigarette between his fingers and burn him; something which his mother seemed to find amusing. That made him rage more at her, evoking an equally savage verbal response that Peter couldn't hear. The simple fact that they had gone anywhere together, especially in the middle of the day when his father was usually hard at work seven days a week, indicated that something was definitely wrong. As his mind wandered, some sense of danger penetrated its way into his head, and he looked up to see both of them looking directly at him.

An escaping gasp made him jump, realising too late that it was his own, and Peter froze as his body decided whether to run or not. His head took over just in time, telling him that he had nowhere to run to.

His body reluctantly followed those instructions and he stepped sheepishly out from behind the house to the sound of cars doors opening and slamming.

"What the hell are you doing here?" his mother screeched at him.

"Don't you lie to your mother, boy," his father warned; his voice heavy with the unspoken threat of physical punishment.

"School closed," he blurted out as he retreated, eager to instinctively stay out of striking distance, "they sent us all home."

Pater's parents looked at one another in silence, as though the information made sense to them when it didn't make any sense to him at all.

"Get inside," his father eventually snapped at him, seeming to consider whether to clip him around the head just because. Peter went inside. Following the automated responses for getting in from school, he ran up the stairs to remove his uniform and fold it neatly ready for the next day, failing to understand that there wasn't ever going to be another day at school. He dressed in some rough clothes and, as much as he hated to be anywhere near them, went downstairs to ask what was going on.

~

That evening, sitting in darkness in his room after the reward of an early bedtime yet again, for no reason other than asking questions which remained unanswered, Peter tried to make sense of what he had been told and what he had seen on the news. There was something going on in London, and as of that lunchtime, nobody was reporting from the city at all.

He had been there once, for a funeral he later realised, but at the time he'd blocked out the arguing from the front seat and stared in awe out of the window at the complete opposite of a world he knew. Everywhere was drab and concrete, with buildings taller than the biggest trees he had ever seen, and the air seemed to have a thicker quality that was totally at odds with the fresh farm breeze he knew. Now, imaging those same streets from the depths of his memories, he struggled to envisage those buildings burning like the ones on the clips of camera footage, and those streets full of people running and screaming. He couldn't get the images he had seen out of his brain. He knew that sleep just wasn't going to happen, so he decided to risk the wrath and try to listen to the television, which was still blaring loudly on the ground floor below.

Creeping as slowly and lightly as possible, Peter slipped out from under the covers and opened his door as softly as he could. The slight creaks and groans from the hinges made him freeze, ready to jump back into bed and pretend to be asleep if he heard even the slightest indication that he had been detected.

Getting the door open enough to slip through, he made his way cautiously to the stairs, keeping his feet carefully to the edges of the floorboards, where they were the least likely to make the sounds which could get him caught. For a moment, he stopped at his sister's bedroom door, and his bottom lip began to tremble as he saw her prized poster of Madonna. He'd laughed at her singing *Into The Groove*, using her hairbrush as a microphone. He made himself look away and carry on, knowing deep down that he would never sit with her on a Sunday evening and record the songs they loved from the charts on their ancient tape deck.

Making painstakingly slow progress in the interests of silence and self-preservation, he crept down the stairs until the partly-open door to the lounge showed him half of the television screen. His father's slumped shoulders were visible in the armchair; the balding head lolled to one side, making Peter imagine the soft snoring that came from him in that position, especially when the mostly empty bottle rested against the side of the chair. He couldn't see his mother, but his mind filled in the blanks and put her sitting out of sight, with a cigarette in one hand and a glass in the other as she stared at the screen with dry, vacant eyes. At least it was the news and not his mother's favourite rubbish, *Dallas*. She spent hours with her glazed eyes glued to that, or worse, her videos of it over and over again.

Satisfied that his father was asleep and his mother couldn't see him – if she was even conscious at all – Peter settled himself down carefully to watch and listen as the television told him the things that *they* would not.

"...declared a state of emergency. Once again, an infectious disease has spread from a London research laboratory and infected the population. Police and military personnel are containing the outbreak, and residents are urged to stay in their homes until instructed. Anyone suspected of being in the early stages of infection, usually denoted by bites or scratches from those already afflicted, should be isolated and avoided. Do not attempt to treat people suspected of being infected. We repeat, *do not* attempt to help people who are infected. Other signs indicating infection are fever, confusion and dementia, and uncharacteristic aggression."

Peter sat still on the stairs, eyes wide and mouth hanging open. It was normal for his parents to drink themselves into oblivion each night, but he imagined that even normal people would be doing that now. He knew London was a long way away, but he was still worried that this illness would sweep across the country and find their little patch of nowhere.

Peter went back to bed as stealthily as he could, and lay staring at the dark ceiling until he drifted into a fitful sleep.

~

Professor Grewal tried to calm himself with mathematics. Calculations and estimates passed the time, and he forced himself to work through the mental arithmetic slowly, step by step, to while away the hours. For the first time in weeks, he felt trapped underground in the laboratory that had never made him feel claustrophobic before. But before, he had been able to simply walk out.

Well, maybe not simply walk out, he admitted, thinking of the security doors and main entrance that was monitored by three guards, day and night. Those guards would not open the airlock doors with their spinning metal wheels until identification was verified via the closed-circuit television feed, but even before all this went wrong he could still, with relative ease, get outside.

Not that he had in weeks, because he had been close to a breakthrough. He had been on the verge of it ever since the two American scientists had come in with their most recent research. But the way the two men with their matching glasses and similar government-issued wardrobes always glanced at one another before answering got on his nerves no end. Their research, conducted under the guise of medical testing and treatment, had been brought across the Atlantic for refining.

Refining. That was what they called it. Professor Grewal called it weaponising.

Morally, he was against the idea, but practically he knew that if he didn't conduct the final process, then someone else would.

It was a matter of professional pride, not arrogance, but he knew the other people in his field and he knew that anyone else they brought in to do the work would be less effective than he was. He knew that the Russians had just as vast a research budget as the USA and the UK combined, and given that the likelihood of all-out nuclear war was very low, he knew that the two hugely powerful nations would find other ways to wage war in silence.

One way involved people like him. Professors in advanced bio-chemistry with real-world experience comprised a very small portion of the world's population, and when they reached the tip of that particular iceberg they tended to know each other. Of all the others he knew, he was certain that he was the best person to complete the research through to testing in the shortest time.

He had been right, at least about his ability to bring that research off the paper and into the bloodstreams of test subjects. What he had been wrong about, however, was the expected effects of the test.

These test subjects were another moral issue, and a solution had been provided by their American counterparts. Prisoners, unlikely to ever earn their freedom within a reasonable time, exchanged their lives for cash so that their families could see at least some benefit from their existence. Under strict conditions to prevent the spread of the disease, the subjects were restrained on the wheeled stretchers and the disease was administered in carefully measured doses of varying amounts.

The disease itself was naturally occurring, and it had taken the Americans years to breed it into the most severe potency. Still, as potent as it was, the speed at which it progressed was still slow enough that the symptoms could be recognised, and the infected subject effectively quarantined in time to stop a cataclysmic spread.

That was where Grewal came in.

His theories on crossing over disease barriers and combining them had been inspired by his research work on vaccinations. By combining the overly aggressive strain of the rabies virus with the fast-acting meningococcal disease, he had been successful in turning up the dial on the new hybrid disease all the way to eleven.

When the six simultaneous human trials began, the small facility was on full lockdown. Those trials began just as expected, and the first ninety minutes went seemingly without incident. At around the two-hour mark, four subjects began to display symptoms in varying degrees. Grewal made a note on his clipboard, mentally disregarding the other two as having received too small a dose to be effective, and he paid close attention to the one subject who he now knew had received the highest amount. Within three hours, that subject advanced far beyond the effects visible on the others, was writhing in pain and crying out. His skin showed angry, red welts and he complained of cramps and a headache.

By four hours, his temperature had risen to such a level that those standing by to monitor him could feel the heat radiating away from his skin.

By the time that temperature was noticeable, the groaning, crying subjects had quietened and were sweating through their rapid, shallow breathing.

One of his laboratory assistants scribbled a rapid note as their doctor called out the time of death for the first subject, followed at regular intervals for the next two, before something very unexpected happened.

Subject one, his frothing mouth hanging open and his rapidly cooling skin no longer glowing pink, but having turned a deathly pale shade, opened his eyes slowly.

It wasn't the simple mechanical response of a body in recent death to relax each muscle, because the eyelids fluttered open and blinked. The eyeballs, clouded and milky as though cataracts had blinded him, turned slowly left and right as though looking for something.

The chest began to rise and fall gently; each movement of the ribcage expanding and contracting prompted a rasping hissing noise, like wind whistling through a creaking door. The lab assistant who had recorded the time of death for that subject froze and turned slowly towards him, checking that the correct information had been annotated against the right subject. Stepping closer, he bent down to watch the rise and fall of the man's restrained chest, placing his own face next to the subject's, and believing himself safe from the contagion behind his mask and goggles, his eyes grew wide just as the face turned towards him and locked its own milky orbs on the man's. Then it opened its mouth wide and bit the man on the face.

40

Six days later, after the full stupidity of the safety protocols in place became apparent and the sealed doors had been opened to investigate why the facility had stopped picking up the telephone, Grewal was still trapped in the store cupboard.

The lock was holding and showed no signs of changing that dynamic of 'things' outside and him inside, but the supply situation was the more pressing concern. He had no idea what was happening in the wider world above ground, or in fact anywhere other than the three feet of corridor he could see either side of the door he was hiding behind, but his world was a small, dark place.

Not needing to count off on his fingers, Grewal cursed his luck that he had sought refuge in a room without running water and calculated that he had two days before he would be out of fluids and forced to try and escape that room before he was too weak to be effective. The only problem was the two lurching figures outside the door, who responded with blood-curdling screeching noises every time he made any sound. No matter how still he stayed, they would not leave.

He was entombed, effectively, by his own monstrous creation and would soon be forced to fight them or else face a certain, agonising death by dehydration.

Chapter 4

"Well I'm not waiting here for news," Peter's father snarled angrily at his mother, whose only response was to take a further gulp of drink without taking her malevolent stare away from his eyes. He had spent the morning trying to raise people on the telephone, painstakingly dialling each digit of the numbers written in a book and waiting for the dial to slowly spin back to the zero. Each call had either resulted in him slamming the handset back down in frustration at nobody answering or having a terse conversation with the person on the other end. Each time he made a call, regardless of the outcome, it seemed to anger him more.

"I'm going out," he raged, throwing open a door to a cupboard in the hallway and retrieving a shotgun with a belt of cartridges, which he slung over one shoulder, before seeing Peter through the railings of the stairs and glancing back to his wife. He seemed to be weighing something up, like he was searching for the lesser of two evils, before abruptly saying to the boy, "Get your boots on and come with me."

"What are you taking *him* for?" his mother shrieked, waving her half-smoked cigarette at her son as she stalked forwards full of accusations. "Planning on leaving me behind, are you?"

"Don't bloody test me, woman," Peter's father raged back at her, puffing himself up to his full height like a gorilla.

She wasn't intimidated by his animalistic display, and her face told him exactly that.

"Stay here," he instructed her and turned on his heel just in time to ignore the childish face she pulled at him and hear the accompanying huff of derision. A glance at Peter conveyed the information that he should have already got his shoes on and been waiting, so the boy scrabbled down the rest of the stairs to comply quickly.

"Stay," his father added in a growl, this time to their collie dog who had automatically risen to follow at his heel.

Walking at double speed away from the house and towards the farm to keep pace with his much taller father, Peter resisted the urge to ask him any questions. He had learned long ago that asking would only gain the reward of a clip around the ear or a snarled response of an aggressive platitude like, "Listen instead of talking and you might learn something," or, "Two ears, one mouth, boy. Work it out."

So Peter kept silent, and kept pace, as his father strode towards his battered farm pickup with a soggy cigarette hanging from his lips. The once-white pickup was very basic, and he waited patiently until his father sat behind the driver's door and sighed before reluctantly leaning over to lift the pin and unlock the passenger side. Peter slipped in and sat down, trying to keep himself as small and unnoticeable as possible as his father started the rattling, noisy engine.

Pulling out of the drive to the farm he turned right, heading up the lane in the direction of the main road, but stopping at the houses midst the tall pine trees.

"Stay here," he told the boy, not expecting and not receiving any answer, before climbing out and retrieving his shotgun from the flat bed of the pickup. Peter watched him as he walked slowly towards the houses, and he saw the gap that one missing vehicle had left. One of the farm workers came out of his house, and everything about his demeanour said he was apologising. He wrung his hands as he spoke, keeping himself hunched and smaller than the boy's father, which is how people usually acted around him. Peter knew he was a bully. He was worse than Edward ever could be, because he was strong and not just picking on someone smaller than him to feel better. He bullied everyone, intimidated everyone, and if anyone didn't bow down to him, then he forced them away.

Peter turned his attention back to the conversation and concentrated, trying to decipher what was happening without hearing the words. He saw the worker, a small man called Keith, who did most of the tractor driving. He was pointing to the gap where they expected there to be a car, and saw Keith waving his arms in some wild explanation of something. Peter's father seethed. He knew that face, even if Keith didn't, and he knew he'd stopped listening and was on the verge of violence. Keith's eyes kept flickering towards the gun held low in one hand, as though the world was just crazy enough right then that his boss would use it on him.

Without raising the weapon, and without another word, his father turned and stomped back towards the pickup.

Cramming his big frame behind the wheel after thrusting the gun over to the opposite footwell, he started the rattling engine again and pealed out in a drone of high revs. He gripped the wheel tight, his knuckles glowing white with the pressure, and seemed to hold his breath. Peter kept himself still and quiet, being invisible like he knew how when this close to his father, until he eased off the throttle and let out his breath in a long hiss of escaping air.

"Tony's gone," he said, surprising his son, "pissed off last night apparently. His sister rang him from Aldershot. You know where that is?"

Peter opened his mouth to speak, hesitating because he didn't usually ask him questions that he expected an answer to. He took his eyes away from the empty lane to look at his son, making him blurt out an answer.

"No, where is it?

"It's that way," he said, pointing a finger past the young boy's face and making him stiffen in anticipation, "west, towards London."

London, Peter thought, *where the news said the trouble was.*

"His sister is married to a soldier, and she rang him telling him to get out. She would know, if the army has been sent in. He tried to get Keith and the others to leave too, but they wouldn't."

Something in Peter's mind lit up then, as though a circuit had been connected, and he spoke the words aloud before good sense could stop him.

"Yesterday, when we were told that school was closed, none of the children from the base were there and we heard the biggest convoy ever move past..." he said in a rush, trailing off as he waited for the response to come.

His father just eased off the throttle, slowing the pickup and swinging into the farm yard to creak to a halt. He didn't move, so neither did Peter.

"You asked last night what was happening," he said finally, "well there's..." he stopped, rubbing hands hard across his face, "there's some sort of shit spreading across the country. People are going mad and biting each other, then they catch whatever it is and do the same. The bloody *army* is on the streets. That shouldn't happen!" he said savagely.

Peter kept his mouth shut, marvelling that this was the longest he had spoken to his father without him yelling in as long as he could remember. He looked up at him, risking eye contact in the strangeness of the moment. He looked back down at his son, something resembling kindness or even fear in his eyes.

At least it wasn't the loathing Peter normally saw, which made what he said next even more of a shock.

"I don't want anything to happen to you, or your sister, which is why we need to go and get her."

~

The argument between his parents raged longer than usual, and he sat at the top of the stairs even after the inevitable smash of glass. He had changed into his pyjamas as the sun sank, and by the time his hunger had become painful, the raised voices from downstairs had grown so loud and slurred that he daren't venture down there.

From what Peter could gather, fairly easily because they were shouting at each other without a care of where he was and what he could hear, his mother was against the idea of getting his sister back. His father was adamant, and the smashing glass was her answer to his insistence.

Going to bed for the second night in a row with an empty stomach, Peter miraculously found sleep.

~

The following morning, waking to hear nothing from the other bedrooms, Peter reached out to find his school clothes.

Dressed and warm, he crept downstairs to hear muted voices in the kitchen. His father was dressed, drinking something steaming from a cup whereas his mother was wearing a dressing gown, holding a glass and a lit cigarette and still looking as drunk as she did in the evening. Peter's father saw him first, a twitch of his eyebrows his only reaction to him entering the room.

He fetched a bowl and a spoon, keeping himself out of reach and as small as possible, like he always did, then reached out across the table for the cereal.

As he poured fresh milk from the jug on the table, skimmed from the milking tank on the farm that morning as always, they seemed to jointly decide to ignore their son and carry on.

"Right," his father said after draining his cup and pushing back his chair to stand, "I'm off. I'll be back later."

His mother's only response was to huff at him and turn away and stare out over the kitchen sink into the back garden. Peter sank a little lower into his chair, crunching his cereal as quietly as he could. He looked down the hallway, seeing his father pause at the cupboard and replace the shotgun as he evidently thought twice about taking the weapon towards the distant towns and away from the safety bubble of the land they occupied. Without another word or even a casual glance, he went out of the front door and left.

Peter continued to crunch as silently as possible, not wanting to incur the wrath of his mother, who was still staring out of the window at nothing as the cigarette burned a long, drooping stick of ash, which eventually dropped onto the kitchen side. Finishing his breakfast and shooting her a quick glance to see if he was being watched, Peter raised the bowl to his mouth to drink the sweet milk left at the bottom.

She didn't see him, otherwise he would have earned another slap around the head, so he rose and went to wash his bowl in the sink as he always had to. Only she was blocking the way as she continued to stare out of the window. Seeing the slight rise and fall of her shoulders as her face was turned down, it took Peter a moment to realise that she was crying. Not sure how to respond at first, he gently set his bowl down and put a small hand on her arm.

"It's alright," he said nervously, "Dad will come back an-"

"Who bloody asked you?" she snapped as she rounded on him, wearing a furious, red-eyed look of hatred, "get back upstairs and take your school clothes off. You're not going to school again."

Having taken an instinctive step back so as to be out of striking range, he was already half-way to the door, so he turned and fled the remainder of the distance.

"And you can stay up there!" he heard her shriek in her grating voice from the kitchen, just as he could make out the clink of a bottle against a glass.

Back in his room, Peter did as he was told and put his school uniform neatly back where it had been before, and he got dressed in yesterday's clothes. He got out the few toys he owned, either donated or found cheap and second hand when one of them was feeling generous or guilty, and played in silence as he mouthed out the words the figures said to one another.

Lunchtime came and went, as indicated by the blue and red hands of his watch which his sister had taught him how to read, and still no summons had been yelled from downstairs. On his third day of being hungry, he could no longer bear missing a meal and creaked open the door to sneak down the staircase with careful steps.

At the foot of the stairs he paused, still unchallenged, and listened to the sounds. The television was on, as it often was throughout the day and night, but he listened long enough to hear nothing but the sounds of the programme. It was a film by the sounds of it, and one that made him think it was supposed to be funny from the musical noises probably designed to make people laugh as much as the jokes were. Risking discovery, Peter crept to the door and peered around to find her still wearing her dressing gown and sleeping in the grubby chair she occupied and forbade anyone else to sit in. The bottle lay empty on the carpet, and the glass had tipped out of her hand to rest lazily against the arm of the chair.

He retreated silently, stealing into the kitchen to grab slices of bread and scrape a slab of margarine onto each one before stacking them to creep back upstairs. As soon as he got back to the relative safety of his room he ate hungrily and continued to play until the sun sank outside his window. But then, two things happened simultaneously. His belly growled, reminding him that he was still hungry after barely eating for three days, and then his stomach lurched because Peter realised that his father hadn't returned before dark.

Chapter 5

John, father to a daughter and a son, and husband to a vile shrew of a woman who he hated when she was drunk, but despised beyond comprehension when she was sober, had driven sedately towards the big town where the hospital was.

He drove slowly, not through being careful, but because with each mile he travelled he felt himself growing ever more suspicious. That suspicion was caused by a dawning realisation that he hadn't seen another moving vehicle yet. It was very common to never see a moving vehicle, as the only thing down their lane was the farm and it wasn't a shortcut that led to anywhere. But out on the main roads it was usual to pass five or six cars by the time they came to the first buildings. Those buildings, bizarrely a large pub and a small police house, sat side by side and seemed abandoned.

Shaking his head as though to dismiss the twin thoughts of stopping in for a drink and wondering why nobody was there, he pressed on and settled his mind back to the road. Driving in that area didn't take much in the way of concentration, he knew because he drove drunk almost every week without fail, and the chance of stumbling across the two policemen who patrolled their corner of the county was slim.

What also made it easy was that there were usually very few other cars on the road, so giving way to another vehicle was a thing of rarity; so much so that he had to concentrate especially hard if he ever drove anywhere else. And when he did, he was scared if he let his concentration slip, he might just carry on as if he was the only person driving.

That morning though, his belly sour from the previous day's alcohol and the insufficient breakfast, his unease about the road situation was growing in intensity. Not one car, not a single other moving vehicle was on the road. Trying and failing to ignore that fact, he continued through a village which was merely a collection of a dozen houses centred around a crossroads where the road met the rail line, a thatched cottage and a small shop-cum-post office. Deserted. Slowing the car, he saw that the window to the shop was damaged and the heavy plate glass was smashed inwards. Deciding against stopping to investigate, he pushed down on the accelerator to propel the car towards the hospital.

Arriving fifteen minutes later, having seen the same disturbing tale in three other hamlets, he reached the hospital to see chaos, and evidence of a fire at the main entrance. It had been small, otherwise the whole building would have been ablaze, but it had been sufficient to blacken the glass front and prevent him from seeing inside. Ignoring the main entrance in his growing fear, he headed for the side of the main building to drive around to the psychiatric unit out of sight of the main hospital.

——

These things were usually kept away from the public eye, as unsightly reminders of such things weakened a person's resolve.

Finding the single-storey building which he knew was the psychiatric assessment unit, he stopped and slowly ratcheted the handbrake on. He stayed in the car, unable to shake the now obvious sense that something was very wrong but trying his hardest to refuse to believe that any disease or rioting in London could affect them this far away already. He decided that the emergency workers had probably all been drafted in to the capital, and he nodded to affirm that assumption to himself before climbing out of the car and striding towards the doors.

This place, he had been told, would keep his daughter for up to two weeks to do an assessment on her before either sending her home or, more likely they believed, admitting her to an in-patient facility somewhere nearer the coastal towns.

They, or more accurately *he*, had decided to bring her home due to the crisis they had heard about on the news channels. She could be sorted out another time, but it mattered to him that the family stay together on their farm until all that London nonsense subsided; a sentiment very common to people who resided all their lives in the country and had a deep mistrust of such things that went on in cities.

That sentiment, as false as it was, evaporated as soon as he pushed open the doors of the hospital unit.

The receptionist, her white blouse and the pale skin of her face sheeted with dried blood, turned slowly, almost mechanically, around to face him as he walked in.

"Hello," he said gruffly, "I'm here for my..." he trailed away as the horror scene of the woman finally connected with his brain. He said nothing, merely stared at the woman waiting for some kind of explanation which never came. Letting out a crackling noise somewhere between a hiss and a groan, she began to mount the reception desk separating them. Moving one limb at a time like a drunk, she continued to groan in and out, the sound like a comedy impression of a creaking door in a horror film as her eyes stayed fixed on him, unwavering and resolute.

John involuntarily took a pace backwards, then two more as the impetus of the receptionist took her off balance and she fell to plough her face directly into the hard floor in front of him. She didn't react, didn't pause or cry out or waver, she simply reset herself and continued to move towards him. He backed up as far as he could go until his back met the glass doors, which opened inwards and blocked his escape. Letting out a small cry of horror as he tried to push his way outside once again, he froze as the woman stopped and climbed to her feet unsteadily.

Now that she was upright and away from the furniture, his unobstructed view showed that her right calf muscle had been torn almost completely away.

That horrible injury didn't seem to debilitate her, nor did the evident blood loss stop her from stumbling towards him to close the gap to a mere arm's length. Finally, his fear snapping, he threw out a jab of his large fist with all the easy strength of a man who had worked outside his whole life, and he connected with her face. Her nose crunched, her head snapped back on her neck like a slow-motion replay of a car accident, and she toppled backwards to slam into the ground again with a broken nose.

Straightening himself, John shrugged off the confrontation as he rolled his shoulders backwards and told himself that he hadn't been scared after all, and that the woman merely needed putting in her place before she got herself hurt. Just as these foolish, misogynistic thoughts reaffirmed his arrogant belief in his own superiority, the receptionist groaned again and flopped over onto her front, where thick, dark, congealed blood poured like oil from her shattered nose onto the shiny floor. With evident difficulty and poor co-ordination, she regained her feet and shuffled slowly in a circle again to re-acquire John in her sights.

The teeth pulled back from bloody lips, the hands rose up to point directly at his face as though she were accusing him, and she lurched towards him again, hissing a louder groan than before. John curled a lip, knowing that he wouldn't pull his punch this time, and drew back his hand with narrowed eyes as his body rocked back in preparation to deliver a huge blow.

Then he stopped, frozen in wide-eyed terror as he looked into her eyes. Those eyes, he now saw, were clouded over in blindness. They were milky orbs set inside sunken sockets, and the sight of them hit him in the chest with such a stab of fear that he was powerless to move. Some instinctive sense, however, sparked movement in him, and his body took up the backwards rocking motion with greater effort than before to build the power, and his fist raised again to rocket his upper body forwards behind the punch as his hips swung through to deliver the maximum amount of force possible. The crunching noise echoed loudly in the confines of the small atrium, and the woman crumpled backwards like a felled tree. The left side of her face, crushed inwards by the uneven battle between stationary cheek bone and large, rapidly moving fist, was a mess of bone and gore. She didn't get up a second time.

Satisfied in some small sense, if not totally confused and terrified, John straightened himself and stepped over her body. He had no idea that he was stumbling around in shock, that his own mind had created a kind of fortress around itself to protect him and keep him moving, despite the things he had just seen and done, and he had no idea that there was worse still to come.

Pushing through the double doors behind the tall desk, he walked down a corridor and ignored the streaks of brown, dried blood which had filled the air with an almost metallic tang.

He ignored the broken furniture and the cracked windows held intact by their reinforced mesh to prevent the shards from being used as weapons. He even ignored the hissing moans coming from behind the closed doors he passed as his presence stirred up the occupants. Keeping his eyes focused on the end of the corridor ahead where he could see the glass bubble of a nurses' station, he stopped before it to take in another scene that his brain couldn't process. He leaned forward, placing his hand against the glass to shield the light away from his eyes, to peer through the streaked blood and through to the other side.

A hand slapped hard against the glass, making him jump backwards and utter a strangled cry of alarm. The hand, blood-soaked with torn nails and the index finger missing from a ragged wound at the first knuckle, squeaked slowly down the pane as the rest of the body rose upwards into sight.

John's mind, already on desperately thin ice, lost the battle and shattered the remaining fragile protection surrounding his wits.

The young girl, a teenager by her size and build, was sheeted with blood from a gash on her head which obscured her features. Her face tilted to the side in curiosity as it tried again with its ravaged hand to push through the invisible force field keeping her from the living body that intrigued her so much. Blinking involuntarily, the blood wiped away from the eyeballs to show the same blind, milky, soulless things he had seen in the receptionist's eye sockets.

Hitting her hand harder against the glass and finding that it didn't yield, she turned her head towards the door next to her and slowly, shakily, reached out for the handle.

John, his own eyes drawn to the opposite side of the door, stared in horror as the handle began to depress before it flung back upwards as though the slippery hand operating it had lost traction. Hearing the hiss from the other side raise in intensity, he looked on as the handle was pushed down again. Too late, John snatched for it to keep the thing shut inside and away from him, but the door had already opened and a hand shot through the gap to reach for him. He drew himself up to slam the door using all his body weight, only the blood-slickened floor betrayed him and took away his footing. Slamming down to the ground in shock, he looked up just in time to see the thing fall on him, forcing his hands out in front of him on instinct. The girl, chomping her teeth down onto the side of his left hand painfully to pierce the calloused skin of his rough hand, fixed him with her milky eyes.

He froze again, mouth open in pain and horror as the two locked eyes before hers turned away to get a better purchase on him. In that moment, he drew up one foot, placed it into her hip, and shoved hard to send her through the air and back through the doorway. Already on his feet but unaware of getting up, he slammed the door shut and ran the length of the corridor, now terribly aware that other doors were rattling and opening, before bursting out and tripping over the body of the receptionist to fall hard.

Scrambling to his feet again, he wasted precious seconds as he tried to push open the doors to the outside world before his brain took some semblance of control and he pulled instead to be instantly rewarded with fresh air. Running to collapse against his car, he looked at the neat row of teeth marks crimping the outside of his left hand, which already welled with blood and seemed to be turning the skin surrounding it grey.

Fumbling for his keys, he tried to start the car to return home, to tell his wife that the hospital staff had gone insane and blind and they had bitten him, but the weakness and dizziness and nausea took over, making him slump over the wheel into eventual unconsciousness.

Chapter 6

The sun set fully, and Peter heard movement downstairs. The drink had obviously worn off, and he heard the downstairs toilet flush as the pipes in the bathroom opposite his room gurgled in echoing answer. The familiar clink of glass on glass travelled upstairs, making him feel less than hopeful for a meal that evening. He was starting to feel really hungry, to the point that hunger was almost overriding the sense of dread he felt at being left alone with his mother. That concept alone was terrifying enough, but when added to the knowledge that his father was supposed to be back by then with his sister, it made the boy's heart drop.

If his sister came back, at least he would get some food cooked for him, and he would probably get told more of what was going on. If she didn't come back, then feeling hungry all the time was probably going to be the least of Peter's worries. That his father hadn't returned was also a concern, but not as much as being left alone with the evil witch.

Peter and his sister used to play, safely away from the house in their secret den underneath the low branches of the pine trees, pretending that they'd been adopted by an evil step-mother who hated them. He thought that those games were just her way of helping him come to terms with their situation, and she always promised that as soon as she was old enough she would leave and take him with her.

Peter's sad reverie was burst like a balloon by noises firing up the stairs like a rifle crack.

"Get down here! Now!" she screeched up at him, making his legs respond with an instant obedience borne of fear to lift him from the carpet and towards the door before his mind had even comprehended the order. Peter scurried to the stairs, stepping down them one at a time and slowing with each step as she waited at the foot with her hands on her hips and a scowl on her face. She waited until the boy had reached the bottom step and paused before pointing with a single finger to the carpet directly in front of her feet.

As instructed, and careful not to show any reluctance or fear, Peter stepped forward, anticipating the clip around his ear which usually came with the orders to step within range of her.

"What do you want to eat?" she snapped, a heavy hint of reluctance in her voice, as though she fought against her instincts to both nurture and abuse him at the same time.

"Anything," he said quietly, hoping that was the right answer.

"Anything?" she sneered back at mockingly, "*anything* isn't a meal. I asked what you wanted."

As she spoke, that sickly-sweet fermented smell of alcohol hit him. He fought hard to keep his face neutral as his eyelids fluttered despite the battle to keep them still.

"Pasta?" he tried, hoping that would assuage her anger at his previous incorrect answer.

She huffed, reluctantly allowing that as an acceptable response, and stalked away to the kitchen where she picked up another cigarette from a packet and lit it from the burnt-down nub between her fingers. Given no further instructions, Peter stepped gingerly into the lounge where he perched on the edge of the itchy, brown settee and watched the television screen. The program showing was saying nothing about what was happening, and he stood to switch the channel after first turning down the volume so that the sudden change was less likely to be noticed. Pressing in the first button on the top left of the control panel, which was unmarked but that he knew was for BBC One, Peter walked backwards to the settee again to watch the static logo on the screen and strain to hear the words.

"…stay in your homes, do not interfere with military operations and do not try to attend hospitals if affected by the disease. You are advised to stay in your homes, do not interfere…"

The recording looped again, repeating the same information over and over.

What kind of disease was it? Peter thought. *Why can't you go to hospital if you're ill? Isn't that the reason for hospitals?*

"What do you want with it?" came the shout from the kitchen, making Peter jump.

"Cheese," he answered, adding "please," before he earned punishment for poor manners.

Grumbled noises came in response but nothing which required him to move or answer, so he switched the channel again. On the third button he found a live broadcast, or at least not a sound recording on loop. This one had a man in a suit and with a moustache that was distracting when he spoke. He looked slightly dishevelled and very uneasy, scared even, and his eyes kept flickering away from the camera to look around the studio that wasn't shown on the screen. He shuffled some papers on the desk in front of him and asked someone behind the camera if they wanted him to go again, then he nodded when he got an answer, before clearing his throat and trying to make his face serious and commanding.

"Good evening, and welcome to the ITN News. An epidemic is sweeping the streets of Britain, after it was inadvertently released from a London laboratory, we believe late last week. Experts state that the mysterious illness causing the chaos is similar to the rabies virus. Those affected by it display extremely aggressive behaviour towards others, and there have been numerous incidents of…" the eyes flickered again before the throat was cleared a second time, "incidents of cannibalism. Transmission of the illness is also believed, experts claim, to be via bites and saliva from the infected. The London Metropolitan Police Force made a statement yesterday urging everyone to stay in their homes and not to interfere with the efforts of police and military personnel. Footage from the capit…"

The screen suddenly went black, shrinking to a slowly dying dot of white in the very centre of the box, just as loud swearing came from the kitchen.

Power cuts so far away from the towns were a regular thing for the farm, but the timing of this one made Peter jump. He could hear the sound of drawers being pulled open and slammed closed from the kitchen, making him think that she was looking for candles to light and carry on with the meagre meal preparations. It was only really the lights which ran on electricity, as the heating and cooking was fuelled by the large oil tank outside. Because that was apparently expensive, the heating was rarely used. Peter wondered the last time he was told not to even think about turning the fire up, how much their endless supply of oil cost.

The television screen was in total darkness now, the tiny dot of residual light faded into nothingness, and he was left in the dark room alone without any link to the outside world.

"It's ready," came an annoyed shout from the kitchen, and he stood to walk fast into the other room where he took a seat at the table, to be presented with a messy pile of undercooked pasta and not enough grated cheese to match it. He ate in silence, being watched the whole time as she smoked her way through three cigarettes until he had cleared the plate.

"Please may I get down from the table?" Peter asked meekly but with enough confidence to hopefully avoid any accusation of mumbling.

She nodded once, so he stood and carried his plate and fork to the sink where he began to run the water to wash them.

"Oh, just leave that," his mother snapped out of annoyance as she waved her hand in his direction, "I'll do it, you just go to bloody bed."

He went without a word, and much later as he lay awake, Peter thought he could hear her crying downstairs alone.

~

Waking the next morning, Peter did as he was told and didn't put his school uniform back on. Instead he wore the same clothes as he had been wearing the day before. They weren't dirty, nor had he been wearing them for long enough to fall into that immeasurable bracket of 'dirty enough to wash'. He went downstairs to find that she hadn't risen yet, so Peter let the dog out of the back door where it whined pitifully, and slipped his feet into his boots to follow.

The morning air was brisk but not cold, but that wasn't what made his brow furrow. It was something else; it was the noise of the morning which was wrong. Normally, there would be some sounds from the farm, and the absence of those regular noises felt alien. Not that the morning was silent, but instead of the distant hum of the dairy machinery working for the morning milking session, there was the constant and distressed cacophony of cows.

His young brain recognised that they should have been milked by now, as that process started when the sky was still just in darkness at this time of the year, but their braying complaints rolled across the yard behind the house to spell something very out of sorts. Deciding that his father wasn't in a position to reprimand him for going over there, seeing as he was starting to realise that he was probably never coming back, and that his mother was still sleeping off the bottle or two she had gone through the day before, Peter walked to the gate and made his way on to the farm, with the dog trotting easy circles around his slow progress.

Finding the milking parlour in silent darkness, something that the power cut shouldn't affect, given that it had its own generators as testimony to how often the electricity grid failed their remote location, he carried on past towards the sound of unhappy cows. Creatures of habit, all the black and white cows with their heavy, swinging udders all crowded in the field at the gate, expecting it to be opened and to file in to be milked and fed. Peter doubted whether they really understood what happened each morning and why, but even a creature as simple as a cow can understand a routine.

He knew then, that with his father gone, none of the others would work on the farm. One had already left, he knew that much, but the others had either quit without telling anyone or had also abandoned the farm.

Or worse, he thought, before he banished that thought from his head, *but that can't be, can it? That's in London and it's miles and miles away from here.*

Walking back to the house, Peter had been back inside for less than a minute before he heard the sounds of her walking down the stairs, surrounded by the cloud of her first cigarette of the morning.

Chapter 7

Peter's life evolved into something resembling more freedom than he had ever enjoyed, but the cost of that was a crushing loneliness which gathered more force daily. The knowledge that his father and sister weren't going to come back escaped his young mind most of the time, and he found that he allowed his thoughts to force the facts that he didn't want to recall out to the fringes where they could be almost ignored.

He filled his days with walks on the farm, sometimes with the dog at his side; not out of any loyalty to him but another force of habit that dictated its place was outside. The dog was no pet and seemed to ignore Peter most of the time as it clearly felt its own spot on the family hierarchy was well above Peter's own. Only now, with the father and the dog's master gone, did a reluctant companionship emerge between the two.

That bubble of freedom was burst after four days, when his mother woke him with her screeching voice from downstairs as she raged and broke things. Pulling up the covers a little tighter, he hoped that she would contain her rage to the ground floor and not remember him.

~

Early on the fifth day that they were alone, Peter woke to a sensation that something was wrong.

His eyes fluttered open; first the left and then the right until the bright light streaming in through the open curtains was manageable. The thing that was wrong, as he realised with sudden fear and panic, was his mother standing in his room wearing an exasperated look of hostility. She picked at her nails, something she did when she couldn't smoke, and her red-ringed eyes bored into him menacingly.

"Get up," she snarled, "we're going out."

Doing as he was told, he dressed under her watchful and malevolent gaze, then tried to inch past her in the doorway. She did this often, blocking his way to force him to ask – to beg – for her permission to pass.

"Excuse me, please," he said in a humble voice.

"Speak up," she snapped at him.

Raising his eyes in defiance, then as his nerve abandoned him at the last minute, he dropped his gaze and asked again in a louder voice that still showed what he hoped would be enough deference to avoid being hit.

She smirked unkindly and stepped aside to allow him enough room to get through the gap by her elbow. As he passed, she leaned sharply towards him and caught the side of his head with the elbow, as though it was his fault.

Numb to the pain and almost immune to her bullying tactics after years, Peter regained his footing and walked to the bathroom where he did what he needed to do and brushed his teeth afterwards. Realising that breakfast would obviously be bypassed, he was hustled out of the front door and towards the farm.

She shoved him in the back towards the battered pickup, as their family car was now missing, and she fumbled with the unfamiliar keys to get in. Spending almost a minute adjusting the seat back, she left him standing outside the passenger door until she reluctantly leaned over to let him in. Settling into the seat and making himself small and insignificant, he pulled his seatbelt and clicked it home. As the squeaking, rattling engine whined, the pickup bucked slightly as she failed to anticipate how low the clutch was on the unfamiliar farm wagon.

Stopping at the edge of the driveway onto the road, more out of habit than actual care, she paused to look right before turning left to go down the narrow and overgrown track that led to nowhere special.

The roads, as unmaintained and rough as he was used to, bounced Peter around in the passenger seat uncomfortably as his mother mithered and muttered under her breath beside him. He kept quiet and looked out, unable to open the windows to allow in any fresh air because of the overhanging greenery scraping and bumping off the cab intermittently. Staring out of the dirty glass, Peter found solace in doing something and moving somewhere, instead of just waiting at home barely getting fed.

He wanted to ask where they were going, what they were looking for and to quiz her about the reasons, but the risk of her responding as she usually did was too great and would spoil his mood.

He kept quiet and waited to find out the answers to the questions which were too risky to ask. When they reached a T-junction, devoid of any traffic or obstructions, he held his breath as her muttering became louder. Glancing across, he saw how she gripped the wheel with one hand as the other shook almost uncontrollably at her mouth, while she intermittently bit at the nails in between uttering words he couldn't make out. Too scared to move, he stayed still and quiet as he always did around her when she was within striking distance. Without warning, she snarled something to herself and turned right in a chirp of tortured tyres as the pickup bucked with the change from first to second gear. Keeping her foot hard down on the accelerator, she crept the speed up into the next gears, as Peter stayed still and quiet. Slowing after a while, she turned right off the road into a small car park. He recognised the place, having been dragged there in the past to collect their car, or even once in the darkness when his father carried her bodily out of the small brick building.

Their nearest pub, ironically called the Fox Arms, which always made Peter ask the silent question to himself about foxes not having arms, stood quiet and brooding. His mother seemed oblivious to the air of brooding menace the building seemed to give off, as she spilled from the car with shaking hands and a pale visage displaying her annoyance at catching her son's eye.

"Stay here," she said firmly, giving Peter the slight sense that he detected a waver in her voice.

He stayed. He watched her stagger slightly as she made as straight a line as she could manage towards the front door of the building, disappearing inside and leaving him suddenly alone.

His heartrate rising fractionally, Peter scanned his surroundings just past the dirty glass which was all that separated him from the outside world and all of the unknown frightening things which were happening there. Forcing himself to breathe and be calm, he assessed the things he saw and catalogued them. A tall evergreen tree swaying slightly, betraying the wind blowing higher up than ground level. The flashing lights of the railway crossing further up the road, not flashing now as no trains were imminent. The two other cars on the small patch of ground he occupied, both looking cold and still as though they hadn't moved in a while.

Slowly, he dared to wind down the window an inch, stiffening at the squeak the handle emitted when he first took up the pressure, and allowed more senses to come into play to build the picture of his immediate surroundings. Lifting his chin to take in a long breath through his nostrils, Peter added more information to the list.

Birdsong, high in the trees. A slight chill on the breeze, bringing with it the smell of wet woodland which was very different to the wet grassland that was so familiar on the farm. More noises drifted to him then, both familiar and startlingly different.

Glass breaking, muffled by distance and obstructions, but unmistakable. A shout, a bang.

At the sound of the bang, his visual acuity snapped his head to the right and back to the door which he had last seen his mother disappearing into. She re-emerged then, her arms full of clear glass bottles containing liquid that looked like water, but Peter knew was not. In her panicked flight, he smirked as she fumbled one of the bottles held awkwardly in her arms and dropped it, to hop in an ungainly dance over the smashing glass, heard crisply and clearly now. He also heard the string of foul obscenities that spewed from her vile mouth and the smirk wiped itself from his face in case she saw and took her revenge.

From the way she ran, or was trying to run, awkwardly with her arms full, Peter thought that she hadn't paid for the bottles and associated the shouting from inside to mark that theft. His brain registered that he had only heard one voice shout, unmistakably that of his mother, but the omission of other sounds didn't fully paint the picture that she described when she regained the safety of the cab.

"He's fucking nuts, that bastard," she spat as she threw herself in, barely able to perform basic motor functions with her rapid breathing and red face. Throwing the four surviving bottles into Peter's lap, she turned the key and crunched her way into first gear before slamming her right foot down and tearing out of the car park almost out of control.

Revving each gear beyond comfort for as long as Peter could hold his breath, she suddenly slowed and stopped the car on the gravel verge, before fumbling with the sequence of the controls she needed to manipulate, and she stalled the pickup.

Turning furious eyes on him, he snatched an involuntary breath and flinched to shut his eyes tight as her hand shot out towards him.

Opening one eye to confirm what his ears had told him was happening, he stared at her as she sat next to him. Her desperate reach wasn't to hit him, he realised, it was to make a grab for the one thing she needed most. The seemingly life-sustaining liquid in the bottle she now tore at feverishly to remove the screw cap from, and to tip it to her mouth. The roof of the cab prevented her from upending the bottle completely, forcing her to dip her chin and try to make her body smaller in an attempt to force the drink to flow. Pausing, she took three deep breaths to steady herself, then began her frantic guzzling once more, before a lack of oxygen forced her to stop and breathe. Slowly, her hands no longer trembling incessantly, she put the lid back on the now quarter-empty bottle with relative ease and closed her eyes as she let the drink flow though her body, as though she couldn't think or function without it, as if it was the fuel she ran on. Opening her eyes, she turned to regard him and did the rarest of things.

She smiled at him.

He had seen it a few times in his life. Not the smile she cast on him when she was relishing the anticipation of punishing him, but a genuine smile of someone who was happy. Her sudden likeness to his sister stung him deeply, as though without seeing his mother look at him kindly, he had never noticed the family resemblance until that moment.

"That's better," she said glibly, as if simple joviality could cover up her debauched need for the drink, and she thrust the bottle back at him to hold. He took it wordlessly, watching her restart the truck with deft hands and far more poise with the controls.

"Next stop," she announced gleefully, "shop. Hopefully nobody else tries to run me off today."

Peter knew that the shop meant a purchase of a whole carton of cigarettes from the Greek man who owned the franchised chain store with its attached single fuel pump. The local shop, as it was known, was local for a few hundred people spread out over miles and miles of farmland. There was another small shop of the same chain in a village that Peter's bus to school passed through. He could see the same sign, the same flash of three simple colours, on the corner building where the houses of that village met the railway line. The same railway line that he had seen minutes earlier, in fact, just further down that line.

This absent-minded train of thought covered the time it took for his mother, now renewed with a seemingly youthful energy and positive nature, to drive them to the shop.

Getting out, she paused, leaning back down to issue the same growled threat to stay, but then she seemed to hesitate.

"Come on then," she snapped, albeit in a higher pitch than usual, which he guessed meant she was trying to be fun and companionable. Hurrying to release his seatbelt, he spilled from the car to stand upright and move his feet fast to catch her up, if only to hover just out of the reach of her arms.

The forecourt of the shop-cum-fuel station was as deserted as the pub, but that didn't mean anything there, the area being devoid of life at the best of times. He watched as his mother straightened herself, in his opinion a pointless and vain attempt to make an abusive alcoholic seem in any way respectable. She pushed open the glass and metal door to activate the tinkling bell suspended above the frame.

Hovering just behind and beside her, Peter peered into the gloom as he held his breath. The harsh, ear-grating screech of, "Hello?" coming from his mother made him flinch involuntarily, but he focused his attention back on the poorly-lit interior of the shop in time to anticipate any answer.

None came, and he followed her inside.

Chapter 8

Dean Johnson took stock of his Yeomanry squadron of reservists, who were chatting amongst themselves in the big drill hall. He was both annoyed and secretly pleased to have found that none of the squadron's officers had reported for duty, and he wondered if they had even received the call to ignore in the first place, or whether they simply hadn't made it there yet.

He was glad that none of them had arrived, apart from the Major that was, because in his opinion they were either snot-nosed, entitled children who brought their genetically weak chins to dilute his beloved army, or else they were washed-out old Etonians with little to offer other than second-hand officers' mess stories. The Major was the exception to the rule, in that he had been a career soldier who had achieved the highest rank available to an enlisted man, then had his skills and experience recognised with a commission to attend Sandhurst on retirement, where he graduated with the rank of Captain. The Major was the man who effectively ran the unit, along with his trusted Squadron Sergeant Major, as it certainly wasn't the Lieutenant-Colonel, whose only talent was his insatiable appetite for port and afternoon naps, and Johnson looked up to the Major greatly.

That wasn't to say that Johnson wasn't a man who inspired others. A heavy haulage mechanic by trade, he had joined the Territorial Army in his teens as he could never bring himself to give up his lucrative apprenticeship.

By the time his training had been completed in his day job, he had risen to the rank of Corporal and was marked out as a young man capable of much more. When the pull to join the regular army threatened to take him from his civilian life, he could not bear to lose the huge difference in wages between the careers, so he dedicated himself to his territorial unit, and over eighteen years had risen to the rank of Warrant Officer class two and was awarded the high honour of becoming the Squadron Sergeant Major.

Stepping stiffly up onto a small stack of ammunition crates, he cast his eyes over the almost seventy men who had mobilised when called. Less than seventy from a full complement of almost one hundred and twenty enlisted ranks and officers.

It was, he decided, a fairly shit turn-out.

The call was expected by many, so the excuse of men who claimed not to have been informed was unacceptable at the very least. Now, deciding that it was time he called the assembled men to quiet and explained their tasks, he stood tall on the wooden boxes and cleared his throat.

It was a small noise, but he somehow made it echo throughout the large room and cut the air to silence numerous conversations mid-sentence. Almost as one, the men sat or stood still to listen to their Sergeant Major.

"Gentlemen," Johnson intoned solemnly, hiding his excitement at a live mobilisation behind the sheer gravity of the situation, "fall in, sit down, and shut up."

He waited as they did as they were told.

"I'll keep it short," he began, "because you'll be deployed as of sixteen-hundred tonight. Troop sergeants will draw up stag rotas. That said, numbers aren't what they should be, so Four Troop will be disbanded to give full complements to the other three Sabre troops," he said, meaning that of their four main fighting units, only three could be fully manned and sentries would be posted from that evening, "and we wi…"

"Sorry I'm late, chaps," burst a voice from the back of the room accompanied by the bang of a door. The accent dripped with privilege, but as the young man strode into view, Johnson's worst fears became realities.

Second Lieutenant Oliver Simpkins-Palmer was everything Johnson hated in the officer classes. He didn't dislike the officers as a general rule, and certainly respected many that he had met and worked with over the years, but this man was an aristocratic, elitist, stereotypical bloody Rupert who made his peers call him Olly and dropped the double-barrelled name for ease in the military setting and elected to go with Palmer, as was the male tradition in his family.

He had, in Johnson's not inconsiderable experience, been born with a silver spoon very far up his arse, and every word that dripped from him was languid and infuriated the Sergeant Major.

He was a soldier. He had worked hard and earned his place. Palmer however, had been born to the right family, had never known hardship and would never know the value of money as he and his men did.

His older brother, Johnson knew, had joined the army fresh out of university and had graduated Sandhurst, having made a name for himself as an intelligent young officer. He had been posted to the Household Cavalry, and all reports from the men there was that he had grown into a well-respected young Captain who was popular with his men.

Lieutenant Palmer was the opposite side to that coin, who saw the men of the company as beneath him and treated them all as his personal servants. He had also finished university but believed that his career lay in entrepreneurial investments, instead of climbing the ladder through hard work. If Johnson were to believe rumour, which he listened to but didn't read as gospel, then Lieutenant Palmer had inveigled his father into bankrolling his lifestyle, appeasing him by joining the reserves. He seemed to believe that rank, as pathetically junior as his was, offered him privilege far above his earned station.

Respect the rank, Johnson told himself as the annoying twerp strode towards him, *not the man.*

"Mister Palmer," Johnson said through barely gritted teeth as he nodded his greeting to the young man, who stepped close to the boxes he was standing on, "I was just addressing the men, Sir, if you would like to discuss the matter afterwards?" he said, keeping his face neutral so as not to betray the hostility between the two men to everyone.

"I'd like to discuss it before *I* address the men, if it's all the same to you, Sergeant Major," Palmer said acidly, and loudly enough for the closest dozen men to hear.

Johnson stepped down without another word, but wearing a face which indicated a severe level of disapproval. Palmer smiled infuriatingly, forcing Johnson to swallow down his rising anger at the intrusion and control his face, as he strode ahead to the administrative offices with Palmer walking behind.

"Talk amongst yourselves, boys," he called over his shoulder and smiled internally in satisfaction as the ambient noise in the hall rose measurably. Palmer, singling out the nearest enlisted man, spoke condescendingly to him.

"Find me a cup of tea, would you, Smith?" he said annoyingly.

"I'm Parry, Sir," the man answered, only to be dismissed with an irritated wave of the officer's hand.

As soon as Johnson walked inside the office, the door was pushed closed behind him.

In almost mocking contrast of one another, Palmer lounged over the corner of the nearest desk with his legs apart, whereas Johnson stood ramrod straight as though he alone in the room took any pride in soldiering.

"Who gave you permission to address the men?" Palmer asked. Johnson's eyes moved slowly to fix the much younger man, who seemed to lack the courage of his convictions and quailed slightly under the gaze of the tough man.

"Perhaps, *Sir*," Johnson said with an emphasised sneer, "you don't yet know how the army works. Perhaps, *Sir*," he said again, putting yet more aggression into the false deference as he took a pace closer in order that the young man understood him properly, "you don't know how things actually work in this squadron. You might not be aware that almost every decision made is made by sergeants in the HQ troop, or the admin troop or by the Sabre troop sergeants, or, *Sir*, by *me*."

He stepped back and seemed to relax, even allowing a small smile to spread across his face to signify that he meant no more hostility to the new officer.

"In answer to your question, I do not need anyone's authority to address my men. Now, I assume that you would like to know our disposition and orders before I pass them on?"

Palmer, in betrayal of his arrogance, was not cowed by the reprimand and if anything, he seemed to have found the small interaction amusing.

Johnson fought down the urge to slap the man less than half his age and send him to bed.

"Please, *Mister* Johnson," he said with yet more dripping sarcasm than the older man thought possible, "do apprise me of our situation and disposition."

Johnson sucked in a big lungful of air through his nose in order to settle himself and stop him from speaking for a few valuable seconds, then he let it out and spoke.

"Of our six troops, we have a little over half strength,' he began, "I've cut out Four Troop," he explained, meaning that one quarter of their regular fighting units had to be disbanded, "as they have no troop sergeant and no Corporals deemed up to the task of replacing them. Those men have been distributed amongst the other three Sabres and the assault troop, and HQ have been merged with admin for the time being. We still have empty seats, and more vehicles than we have bodies to fill."

"That's all wonderfully explained and I'm sure you can be pleased," Palmer drawled in a voice Johnson could only describe as smarmy, "but I was rather hoping to receive an update about the rest of the country and what's been going on," he finished, his rich and cultured accent bearing a trace of feminine gentility.

Johnson looked shocked, as the man had clearly just rolled up without a clue what had been happening elsewhere.

"Sir," he began, a furrowed brow of concern showing above his shrewd eyes, "London and surrounding areas are *gone*. Wiped out. The entire Household Cavalry unit training at the camp have been deployed to roll armour straight down the bloody M3 into London. We have been mobilised and are on home defence duties effective from six o'clock this evening," he said, intentionally simplifying certain elements of his report, as he doubted the fresh-faced aristocrat could cope with the full truth given in army lingo.

Seeing the mask of smugness slip momentarily from Palmer's face, Johnson went on.

"You know what this is, don't you?" he asked.

"I rather doubt anyone knows what it is, wouldn't you say, old boy?" he responded, infuriating Johnson again at being encompassed in his own lingo and branded as one of them.

"No, I bloody wouldn't," Johnson snapped back, "there's talk of some illness caused by infected animals from France, other rumours about some disease the Americans and the Russians were racing to perfect just so they can keep trying to kill each other quietly, and now there's even the local loonies and god-botherers trooping their own colours and saying it's bloody judgement day."

He took a half step back and calmed himself down before resuming in a more relaxed tone of voice.

"Our job," he explained, "is to patrol and ensure that Her Majesty's peace is kept. We will move down to the training camp and treat it as a deployed forward base. We will keep round the clock defences in place, and we will conduct patrols of the towns and villages. Any questions, Sir?" he finished.

Surprising him then, the younger man removed the look of half-bored amusement from his face and stood up.

"Thank you, Sarn't Major," he said formally, "what about our supply and equipment situation?"

Johnson, as surprised as he was, did not hesitate and nor did he need to refer to any notes.

"Full complement of vehicles," he began, "sixteen Fox armoured personnel carriers, each with a 30mm canno…-"

"I'm aware of our standard armaments, thank you," he interrupted, although with less arrogance than before.

"We also have four Spartans, two Sultans and access to dozens of Bedfords, not to mention the Saxons and whatever else is at the camp," he finished, listing off the troop transport and fighting vehicles at their immediate disposal, as well as the many available larger transport trucks and whatever training vehicles were left behind when the regulars shipped out.

"Ammunition and consumables?"

"More than we can shake a stick at," Johnson answered.

"And contact with other squadrons?" Palmer asked.

"Working on that," Johnson answered, "Lance-Corporals Daniels and Mander are building up a network now, as they have been for the past hour. They'll have got hold of anyone listening by now."

"Very good," Palmer intoned thoughtfully, leaning precariously back towards annoying the more experienced man, "I want to get more information about the situation in the city before we move out. Are we able to make contact with any military units closer to the action?"

The way he said *action* made Johnson grimace inside.

It was like the lustful, youthful way that combat virgins spoke of being in the thick of things, when they had never even held a weapon since their last training weekend.

"Already in hand," Johnson answered, "RNAS Yeovilton are putting up a pair of their training Hawks as long-range reconnaissance in," he looked at his watch, "a little under twenty minutes. We should know more then."

"Outstanding work by all then," Palmer said gleefully, yet still made his words come across as sarcastic and derisive of others' efforts. "Now, who else from the senior ranks has answered the call to arms?"

Johnson stared the young man down until he could keep silent no longer.

"You are the only officer in attendance, Second Lieutenant," he said, intentionally adding the man's very junior rank as a reminder that he should harbour no intentions of taking charge and giving orders.

"Sergeant Major," Palmer said with a clear tone of annoyance in his voice, "I'm starting to suspect that you aren't the slightest bit pleased to see me…"

Johnson now believed that the time had come to explain the facts of life to the man.

"Sir," he said, as kindly as he could manage, "for the sake of clarity, until such time as a Captain or the Major arrive, I'd like to make it entirely clear that this," he stabbed one finger onto the desk to produce a metallic sounding report, "is," another tap, "*my squadron,*" he finished with a final bang on the desk.

Palmer smiled, and Johnson did not feel placated by the gesture one little bit.

"Well, for the sake of good order and pretending for just one blasted minute that Her Majesty bestowed on me a commission, can we agree to include the lowly Second Lieutenant in your hierarchy, even if only to maintain the sense of propriety that the men expect?"

Johnson shot him a look that warned him not to interfere but agreed with a curt nod and a gesture of his chin to follow him back out into the drill hall. Striding straight back to the raised platform of ammunition crates, Johnson stepped up and bawled for silence.

Silence descended immediately, and all eyes turned to him.

"Right then," he called out, "Four Troop, as I said, you have been allocated to the other Sabre Troops. Report to your new sergeants. HQ and Admin troops, you now report to Sergeant Croft. Troop sergeants on me after this briefing."

He paused to clear his thoughts before dropping the news on them. "The capital has been lost to a virus that experts say is like rabies," he paused to let that sink in, casting a fatherly eye over his audience, "and riots have torn the place apart. The Household Cavalry boys have rolled out to stop the riots, and we are back to our original role as home defence. We will occupy the training camp, consolidate and defend, and conduct fighting patrols to quell any incidents." He paused to scan the room once more and waited for the faces to show concern.

They didn't. Most were local boys who would quietly ensure that their families and neighbours would get themselves somewhere safe.

"Alright then," Johnson said loudly, "let's work hard to get away early. Fall out."

Stepping down and walking away with Palmer at his flank, he strode into the room which was being used as a hastily-erected temporary communications suite, just in time to hear Lance Corporal Mander speaking into his radio handset.

"Understood, RNAS Yeovilton, November-Three-Zero out," he said before he carefully put down the handset and removed his heavy headphones. Reaching out to rest them gently on the desk, he suddenly dropped them and flew from his seat to bounce off the Sergeant Major and drop to his knees just in time to grab a metal bin to void the contents of his stomach into.

"Corporal Mander?" Johnson asked, perplexed at the unexpected behaviour.

"The Navy pilots," he said, pausing to spit before he tried to stand and retched again instead, "the Navy pilots have reported back to base," he said as he stood and wiped his mouth on a sleeve.

"And?" Johnson prompted him.

"And they said that everyone is walking the streets in a daze, attacking everything that moves. Except each other, apparently, but Sarn't Major, the armoured column," he paused, his eyes pleading, "they said they were overrun near Southampton…" Mander's eyes bulged again and he threw himself back toward the bin to finish what he had started.

Johnson turned to Daniels and didn't need to ask the question. The other Lance Corporal picked up the headset and microphone to call the Naval Air Station back and seek clarification. Johnson listened to the one-sided exchange, wearing a stoically blank look on his weathered face, his eyes stinging and his stomach doing small flips in response to the smell of Mander's vomit, unable to hear the important parts of the conversation but watching intently as the other man's face dropped in cold horror at what he was being told.

"Sarn't Major," he said weakly, "it's true. The armour has been overrun and the disease has spread well outside London. They said…" he looked down and swallowed, making Johnson think that they might need another bin in the office before long, "they said that the dead are rising and attacking people."

"Oh, good Lord," Palmer said in a higher-pitched voice than normal, "that can't be right. The Navy boys lost their bottle, eh?" he tried. Johnson ignored him, and instead of responding, he strode back out to the drill hall where a gaggle of sergeants awaited him.

"Change of plan," he said with savage purpose, "Andy?"

"Behind you," came a gruff voice belonging to the Squadron Quarter Master Sergeant, Andrew Rochefort. Johnson turned to face him, nodding companionably to the older, shorter man who kept the records of everything they had been or would be issued.

"Every available driver we have takes a vehicle each and we load it with every last supply at this location before we move to the camp. Every bullet, every mortar, every piece of kit, everything down to the last can of bloody beans. Clear?"

They understood him.

"And tell the men to call their families," he said with next to no hesitation, "tell them the disease has spread out of London, and that they should get themselves somewhere safe."

He hesitated again, half turning away before he swung back around.

"No," he said to the small gathering of senior non-commissioned officers, "tell them all to get to the base and bring as much of their own supplies as they can. They can be housed there safely, and we can protect them. Go, now," he said, seeing them all scurry away to bawl out their units and gather their men to them.

"Are you sure that was the right thing to do, old boy?" Palmer's greasy voice wafted over his shoulder, making him turn around to speak in a low voice to the young man.

"How long will the unit stay together when their loved ones are out in the trenches whilst we're safe on camp?" he asked, "How many men will desert to see if their wife or their children or their parents are ok?" Palmer's face finally registered some understanding.

"And," Johnson added icily, "I'm not your *old boy*."

Chapter 9

Peter's experience in the shop was instantly marked as different from the previous times he had been there. There was no music playing. There were no fluorescent lights showing inside their opaque plastic cases which the flies managed to somehow access but never escape. His mother had already scurried her way into the store without pausing to notice anything was wrong with the scene, but her young son was less driven by the need to collect more alcohol and cigarettes than she was.

He watched as she shrieked again in her grating voice, trying to get the attention of the shopkeeper, in vain as nobody appeared to be there. It took her only a few precious seconds to assimilate the facts and weigh up the benefits versus the risks before she began stealing.

Peter heard the noises of bottles clinking together and the almost furious mutterings of an addict not getting their own way easily. His feelings of unease were heightened to almost snapping point when her shrill voice called his name and made him jump clear off the ground. His feet moving without conscious decision, he reported for duty and rounded an aisle to see her with her arms full of bottles and packets and her eyes wide in expectation at him.

"Well?" she snarled, somehow conveying that she was disappointed by his stupidity yet again, "Get a bloody bag or something."

Peter fled, running to the small counter with its barred window that overlooked the forecourt and the single fuel pump standing forlornly, as though the process of someone needing petrol would resurrect it once more to life. Reaching over behind the counter, his hand touched the cool softness of the slab of plastic carrier bags ready to be peeled away by the cashier when needed. Fumbling the first few attempts, Peter licked his thumb and tried again, rewarded instantly with two bags which he struggled to open as he returned to his mother. She told him to hold the bags open, placing one inside the other as she reverently placed the precious bottles inside with more care than she showed to her own offspring. When the bag was full enough to complement the other bottles taken from the pub, but not so full that the greed of an extra litre jeopardised the safety of the first bottles, she abandoned the hunt for alcohol and turned her attention to the cabinet behind the cash desk.

Heading straight for her preferred brand, easily discerned amongst the wall of colour as one of the only packets which were predominantly black, she helped herself to every single packet on display, before hesitating and doing the same with another brand; obviously her second choice. Peter, eager to help and anxious that not helping would attract unwanted attention, licked his thumb again and opened more bags for her to use.

Seeing her greedily making relays to the car as she momentarily left him inside on his own, Peter did the first immoral thing he had ever consciously, willingly done.

On the second time she left him alone for those few precious seconds of solitude, his eyes rested on the shiny, brown packaging of a Marathon bar. His gaze darted up to her receding back as she approached their car, then back to the chocolate.

It called to him. Nestled between the dark blue of the packaging on the Wispa bars and the red, white and blue of the longer but very chewy Curly Wurly bars on the other side. With almost no hesitation, he reached out and closed his fingers around the first Marathon and picked it up. Just as the bell on the front door erupted into horribly loud life to signal the return of his mother.

She looked at him, unaware of what he was doing but utterly convinced that he was up to no good given the look on his face, and she drew back a hand in preparation to slap him around the face. Noticing the chocolate in his hands just before she began the return swing towards him she stopped, relaxed her shoulders, and dropped her hand without warning.

"You could've just said," she admonished him, not for stealing but for looking guilty about it. "Take what you want," and with that, she returned to her relay of ferrying stolen alcohol and cigarettes back to their car.

Peter didn't move.

He still couldn't be certain that he wasn't being tricked, but he reminded himself that everything to have happened in the last week had been more than a little abnormal.

Taking her permission literally, he licked his thumb again and began to fill a few of the thin blue plastic carrier bags with all the things he had never had the courage to ask for. He took pot noodles after seeing the television advertisement for them. He took Cadbury's chocolate, Marathon and Mars bars. He took Caramacs, Star Bars, Toffos, an entire box of Opal Fruits, Yorkies, Sherbert Dips, and filled the three bags entirely from just the shelves below the counter. He took more bags and stuffed them with Monster Munch crisps, Nik Naks, Frazzles, Space Invaders and Chipsticks until those bags were full too. Putting his lighter haul with his earlier heavy one, he turned to get yet more bags and froze as he heard a noise he dreaded.

Outside, the engine of their car was starting.

He threw himself to the door, stopping just in time to snatch his bags up, and dropping one full of chocolate and sweets but not daring to risk the time it would take to retrieve them. Flying from the shop in desperation he arrived at the car in time to see his mother with a lit cigarette in her right hand as she replaced the cap on a bottle with her left.

The cruel smirk of evil she wore on seeing his panic and distress reminded him harshly of the cards he had been dealt in his short life, and he went to climb into the passenger side before his eyes rested on the seat covered in the bags he had helped her fill.

Quickly deciding that she would deem the contents of those bags to be far more important to her than he was, he shuffled sideways and climbed in the back seat. Keeping a wary eye on her as she drove back to the farm, he ate a Marathon in slow silence, relishing every bite of the salty caramel and peanuts inside.

~

Arriving back at the abandoned farm shortly afterwards and having seen no sign of life on the journey back, Peter spilled from the car to loiter out of range of his mother, who had already begun to metamorphose into her old self as the booze coursed its way into her bloodstream. She had become morose and aggressive once more. No doubt now she was able to focus on anything other than her need to get more alcohol and stop her hands from shaking uncontrollably, she recalled the facts.

Those facts, put simply as they were in Peter's mind, were that something terrible had happened in London, his sister and Father had gone and not returned, people were acting weird and had abandoned their farm and, worst of all for him, he was now trapped in their idyllic corner of rural nowhere with his mother, who had descended into an almost catatonic state of self-pity. Almost catatonic, that was, as she still managed to automatically refill her glass with neat alcohol, and chain smoke as she stared holes through the blank screen of the television.

Peter, through seeking solitude and safety from her, took his stolen haul and slipped out of the back door. The dog followed him, not out of any affection or loyalty, but because he was going out via the back door and that was the way to the farm. It was a clever dog, as almost all collies were, especially when they worked on farms, but she displayed no fondness for the young boy and made it clear that her place in life was above his own. Now, for the lack of anything better to do and the subtle promise of food from the rustling bags, it followed him into the chill afternoon.

No sooner had they left via the rear of the house and slipped through the barrier of evergreen trees that stood as the demarcation line between residence and farm, than three shambling figures made their way slowly up the lane from the side least often used.

They had been in a field of waist-high maize, stumbling aimlessly around and attracted by the noise that each other was making. When they moved closer to investigate those noises, no smells inspired their hunger or forced their aggressive natures to surface, so they bumped along almost sightlessly in a trio, looking socially awkward and only friends by default as no others would give them the time of day.

New sounds other than those they made amongst themselves pricked the edges of their automated senses, and made their faces turn as one to the road.

Their feet answered the unconscious call to move towards the sounds and, as one, they shuffled towards the twin barriers of a light hedge and a shallow drainage ditch. That was all that separated them from the rough, neglected tarmac with a strip of insistent grass growing straight up through the middle. One, dressed in the pale blue shirt of a convenience shop franchise, which betrayed the reason for the shop being empty, was the first to fall through the hedge and pitch cumbersomely into the ditch. It did not reach out like a normal person would; there was no instinctive flinch reaction to break its own fall and protect the brain, as humans had evolved to do. Instead, it was merely reaching out ahead of it, as they did to compensate for their reduced visual acuity. That outstretched arm made direct contact in a downward motion, stiffly absorbing the full force of the fall, and a loud crack echoed along the lane and was contained by the tunnel of greenery which enclosed the overgrown passage. The shoulder of that arm disfigured horribly, the lower arm shortened in an instant and a bright shaft of splintered white bone appeared through his mottled, olive skin just before the elbow.

Showing no reaction to the open fracture of his right arm, nor the broken collar bone which grated the two ends together noisily, or the dislocated shoulder, the man in the pale blue uniform shirt clambered awkwardly back to his feet to lead the other two, who were more fortunate.

Shambling as a trio, as a small pack of hungry yet uncoordinated predators, they made their halting, jerky way along the narrow lane in search of the thing that had driven past and made the big noise.

The other two, a younger woman with the same skin tone as the leading one, and an older man of far greater girth, stepped dutifully along in flanking positions as the three made their slow progress onwards. They knew no passing of time, felt no pain and experienced no conscious thoughts about their actions, they just moved resolutely and implacably onwards.

Looking on, it appeared as if someone had managed to coordinate the actions of drunks and herd them all towards a specific point, and all with the same intent. The thing that herded them was the draw of sound, and the intent that their sub-conscious, base-instinct-level brains associated with sound was food.

But food was a by-product. A construct of the disease which inhabited their bodies and took over control for its own ends. A virus has one simple goal in its existence, one mindless, relentless objective which consumes everything: the task of spreading itself.

The virus made the people it had infected associate sound and movement with healthy people.

When close enough, that healthy flesh was pungent in their nostrils and whipped them into a frenzy, when their actions became more intense and their need for food made them desperate, and with that desperation came a sudden and brutal speed and strength that made them display the obvious signs of the disease on which it was originally based. They foamed at the mouth as the over-active salivation glands made their mouths drool and their gnashing, chomping teeth, moving incessantly in anticipation and expectation of human flesh, frothed that spittle into a foam.

But that hunger was a ruse. It was a feint. A fake, a lie, a fiction, a falsehood, a trick; a fabricated deception designed for one purpose, and one purpose alone.

To infect as many more viable hosts as possible.

Chapter 10

Peter pumped his legs to move himself fast over the low, rolling landscape behind the prison of his home. He had paused only long enough to snatch up one of his most valued possessions: a battered camouflage backpack with an army surplus water bottle attached. He filled the bottle from an outside tap, stuffed his stolen haul into the bag and paced quickly away from what he felt was the most dangerous place he could be in.

He'd seen her like this before, when his father was away for something he was too unimportant to be told about, and his sister had called it a meltdown.

Meltdown, he thought, *that's about right for her.*

His only priority was to get himself away from the risk posed by her imminent detonation as soon as the alcohol took over, or the cigarettes ran out, or even something small such as a stubbed toe or a spilt drink set her off. When she flipped, she had no way to regain control of herself. He had learned that to his detriment years before, and as a result had learned to make himself small and invisible whenever he was around her. He decided that, after the look in her eye when she silently threatened to drive away and leave him behind, being around her any longer that day would not end well.

She showed a distinct inclination towards cruelty when she was upset, and she was clearly upset.

Peter had no desire to listen to her ranting become louder and less intelligible before she demanded that he come to her, and stand close enough to be shouted at, and hit whenever she felt like making a point.

He couldn't articulate all of this himself, not easily, but he had the instinct of a survivor to escape potential trouble when he sensed it coming.

It was a different kind of trouble coming, but he had no way of even beginning to understand that just yet.

Instead of watching his mother drink herself into angry oblivion, he walked fast towards the nearest woodland bordering the farm and wove his way between the trees until the early afternoon light was obscured by the heavy foliage. Selecting a fallen log as a seat, he slipped one arm out of the strap of his backpack and swung it around to the front of his body. Selecting himself a packet of crisps he hadn't had before, ones that promised tangy tomato goodness, he settled down to enjoy them one by one.

He was watched intently by the dog, Meg, and her intelligent black and white face fixed on his as he chewed slowly. He had never made a connection with the dog, mostly because the dog had never wanted his attention or affections, as it simply wanted to spend its life on the farm doing what it had always done. Perhaps intelligence or instinct told the dog that things had changed and were never going to return to normal, so she had decided to pay him some attention.

Either that, or the dog was following that universal calling of a rustling packet.

Peter threw the dog one of the ball-shaped corn snacks dusted in the tasty red powder that made his tongue tingle. The dog caught it effortlessly and chewed twice before rejecting his offering by opening her mouth wide towards the leaf-covered ground and making a retching, coughing noise to spit it out. Looking up at him again, her eyes seemed to request an alternative, or at the very least a second opinion on the packet he was close to finishing.

He said nothing, instead ripping open the packet to lay it flat and allow the dog to inspect the residue in its own time. Reaching out a hand to stroke the dog's head, he recoiled instantly as it snapped its hard mouth at his fingers in disgust at his attempt to show affection. She made it clear that she had no interest in his attentions.

Moving on to another bag to select a chocolate bar, he settled on a Spira and peeled open the wrapper to remove one of the twisted tubes of chocolate, and enjoyed them both, one after the other. His stomach, unused to the richness of the high-sugar snacks, turned on him quickly and made him feel sick. He slowly closed up the bag and rose to reluctantly return to the farm, just as a noise rolled over the gently undulating countryside to fight through to his senses.

The cattle were bellowing again, all of them in pain with full udders which they could only associate with their twice-daily milking sessions that came with easily obtained food.

Peter was powerless to help even one of them, let alone the whole herd. Somehow the noise made him fearful, made him feel an urgent need to seek the dubious safety of his house and bedroom. Starting off at a fast walk back towards the cluster of buildings, he heard another sound.

It was distant, but very distinctive. It was, unmistakably, his mother screaming in fear and pain.

~

Just as Peter had predicted, she had drunk at a fast rate, along with her incessant smoking. Within an hour of returning home from the stressful journey of necessity, her hands had stopped shaking and the sharp, stabbing pains in her head had abated. With the disappearance of those physical symptoms, so did other indicating factors of her severe alcoholism dissipate. Her watery peripheral vision had come back into focus, and the ability to concentrate had hazily returned to her, only to be lost once again as the steady intake of more alcohol robbed her of various faculties.

She had drunk so much in such a short space of time that the effects caught up with her rapidly, and when the last cigarette of her second packet burned down to scorch her fingers, she swore out loud. As she swore she dropped the cigarette, and her inevitable flinch at doing so knocked over the bottle to spill the contents and make her swear even more loudly and savagely.

The resulting coughing fit made her lose bladder control momentarily, and that was when she made her way, awkwardly and desperately, to the downstairs toilet where, on her return journey, in eagerness to return to her rum and cigarettes, she saw the three people trying to get through her front gate.

Setting her face and trying to raise herself to a more dominant height, which was difficult for her at a shade under five feet two, she snatched open the front door and let rip with a string of aggressive demands, wanting to know just who the bloody hell they were and what the bloody hell they wanted.

The three bumbling, uncoordinated bodies stopped and turned towards her. Six milky, near-sightless eyes fixed on the blurry shape that had made the noises, and they locked in their other senses. As one, the three of them took long, exaggerated breaths in through their noses, then seemed to stare straight through her and let out three hissing moans of pure, lustful hatred.

Abandoning her designs on any confrontation, she stepped smartly back inside and shut the flimsy glass and wood door to create a barrier between her and the monstrosities clawing at her front garden fence. Now that her mind was a little more focused, and now that the sobering effect of fear had made her senses that little bit more accurate, she noticed that a number of things about these people weren't quite right.

The one at the front, not that she would recognise him as the man who had personally sold her thousands of cigarettes from the shop she had so recently looted, had a badly broken arm and his right shoulder slumped at an unnatural angle. She couldn't make out any clear details on the other two, but she guessed that they too must have the same spotted and mottled skin that reminded her of the pallor she had seen on the very old.

And the recently deceased.

The one at the front, thrashing now in what seemed like an increasingly angry and agitated state, was frothing at the mouth and she heard the sickening snap, snap, snap of his teeth as the lower cracked up on the top row noisily. Deciding very quickly that she wanted none of that nonsense, she stepped backwards again to regain the house proper, and closed the front door to the porch to obscure the intruders, now with the added protection of the wavy glass. Perhaps distortion and protection were interchangeable in her drunken, fearful state. For added measure, she pulled the curtain across and went back into the lounge to do the same and to retrieve her most important possessions. As she lit a cigarette and reached for the glass containing a precious gulp, a splintering, crashing noise rippled outside, making her snatch back the curtain to see that the fence had not held against the combined weight of the three people.

Suddenly worried, as though her brain had finally caught up with the wave of reality washing over their home, she remembered that she was supposed to be responsible for more than just one person.

"Peter," she gasped to herself, then turned her face up towards the ceiling and bawled his name. When no answer came from inside, and she heard only the rise in intensity of the hissing and moaning as the first of six hands banged onto the single pane glass of the lounge window, her face contorted in rage. She stomped off to climb the stairs, only to find her son, her only remaining child, the last person in her family to have still been with her, was gone.

She wasn't sure if she wanted to punish him herself, or whether she actually had any sense of parental care for her own offspring, but either way, she burst from the back door in a fearful rage, and she propelled herself forcefully across the rear lawn towards the gap in the trees where she knew he always slipped through. Stopping in her tracks, she remembered too late the shotgun that her husband had left behind when he had insisted on his fool's errand, and she turned on her heel to fetch it. No sooner had she reached the rear patio than the hissing sound reached her ears again and pulled her gaze sideways to unveil the three people rolling inexorably around the building line and making straight towards her.

As drunk and as useless as she was, there was no escaping that part of her brain that had evolved beyond her cognitive control.

She assessed the threat, turned and fled before she had drawn a breath or even begun to compute what was happening. Her right hand shot out as she ran and clasped the wooden handle of the nearest thing she could use as a weapon, before she jumped up a small flight of three stone steps and rounded on the leader, yelling triumphantly before thrusting the four tines of the pitchfork into his chest as far as they could go.

The savage, animalistic look of dominance and exultation melted from her face as she finally understood that her fatal blow had not been fatal at all. In desperate panic, she withdrew the weapon and buried it into his chest once again, this time feeling the scraping resistance of bone and sinew but skewering him just as effectively. Still, he did not react, did not fall down or cry out and, most worryingly, he did not die.

That last realisation gave her another burst of adrenaline, almost as much as her sedentary body could handle, and she pushed hard onto the tool to force the three bodies backwards down the steps in a pile of reaching, mottled-skin limbs. The smaller one at the back, a woman whose dirty neck and face Peter's mother noted surreally, fell awkwardly, and the sharp corner of a stone ornament crushed the base of her skull just above her filthy neck. The other two, however, as ungainly as they were, struggled to their feet to further induce horror in the woman who now stared up at them in wide-eyed terror.

As one, the two remaining men fell on her, just as she skipped smartly backwards and raised the pitchfork again. The momentum of her attackers, mixed with a healthy dose of good luck, forced the pitchfork upwards where one of the tines found less resistance in the right eye socket of the fatter one who had regained his feet first. As a result, his now inanimate body slumped backwards to pin the man with the broken arm and keep it trapped through a simple weight advantage.

Just as she fell to her knees and erupted in fits of hysterical sobbing, the broken arm shot out and dragged her forwards by her clothing. Feeling her uncontrolled fall towards the feverishly gnashing teeth and wild, dead eyes locked onto her, she screamed fit to wake the dead.

Chapter 11

Johnson's Yeomanry squadron rolled out their first troop, assault troop, inside of thirty minutes from when his orders were given. They were the only troop not to have been given logistics duties and were left fully manned with their four Spartan tracked combat reconnaissance vehicles brimming with men and weapons. They were basically a small, light and lightly armoured tank designed to move the troopers into harm's way in relative safety.

They reported back within two hours that they had arrived at the base unhindered, and they were currently convincing the Royal Military Police guard left in situ that they were under orders to occupy the camp.

"They're asking to speak to our squadron OC," Sergeant Maxwell reported via radio, an air of expectant hope in the statement. Luckily for Johnson, Second Lieutenant Palmer was within earshot of this exchange and cleared his throat.

"I'm sure you have more important things to be doing, SSM," he drawled, "perhaps you'd like me to smooth this one out?"

The way his aristocratic boarding school had taught elocution made his pronunciation of the last work crinkle up and down Johnson's spine like an electrical current, but he nodded his gracious assent for the young officer to try.

Do something useful for a change, he thought to himself harshly, *or at least try.*

Turning away, he heard the accent dialled even higher up the line of ascension to the throne as Palmer demanded the name and rank of the RMP in charge of the tiny garrison troops. Johnson left the room and the berating voice behind as he stepped back out into the large drill hall to see an impossible scene of mass organised chaos.

"Sergeant Croft!" he snapped loudly, looking to locate the man now wearing two hats, as so many of them were, because he was now nominally in charge of both the headquarters troop and the administration troop. A lot of the admin troop had been sequestered by the second highest ranking NCO in the squadron, Rochefort, who was affectionately known amongst the men as The Frog.

The distinction being 'known as' and not 'called'.

Similarly, much of the HQ troop business was now being run by Croft's senior Corporal, a man who was naturally being developed to take Croft's place if and when he left the troop.

Rochefort and Croft were standing only a few feet away from him, and both stepped to his side.

"Where are we with the Bedfords?" he asked the men.

"We have ten fully fuelled and being loaded," Rochefort answered, "there's less ammo here than at the camp, as you'd expect, but I think we'll have it all loaded within the hour."

"Drivers?" Johnson enquired, switching his gaze to Croft.

"All sorted," he said as he glanced down at the clipboard in his hand, which seemed to bear no information relevant to either the question or the answer. "Most of the trucks will have an additional man on board for protection too."

"Does that leave the Foxes short?" Johnson asked.

"Well, yes, but if we are just going..." Croft's answer trailed away under Johnson's implacable gaze.

"Perhaps we should put those men allocated to defensive duties back into the armoured cars," Johnson said amiably. "Who knows? Perhaps if we do need to defend, then maybe having a gunner on a 30mm cannon would be more effective than a single trooper with a rifle. What do you think?"

The tone of voice, although conversational, told Croft precisely what he needed to do and quickly.

"Right," Johnson said changing the subject, "have all the troops made a phone call yet?"

"They've been instructed to, as ordered," Croft answered, a slight look of disapproval flashing across his face, which was rapidly brought under control. Johnson saw it, but also saw the man's eyes dart to Rochefort's and saw the slightest shake of the quartermaster's head.

"Carry on then," he told them as he strode away, only to have Lieutenant Palmer fall in beside him. Stifling his repulsion of the boy, he forced himself to be cordial.

"Everything straightened out at the base now, Sir?"

"All ship-shape now, Mister Johnson," he replied with a shovelful of upper-class glee, as though berating the lower ranks had restored his faith in the propriety of the world. "Their senior man is a Sergeant, but that's not what I need to talk to you about…" his lowered tone and lack of gusto grabbed Johnson's attention, and he stopped to look at the officer.

"They sent out a force of thirty," he said in a conspiratorial voice, "last night. They intended to recce the routes to the main roads, look to establish observation posts and the like, but none of them returned. Got the chaps left behind feeling a little jumpy, I think."

Johnson's eyes went slightly wider, then narrowed.

"And they didn't make radio contact? Didn't go after them?" he asked pointedly.

"It seems not," Palmer told him, glancing left and right to ensure his words weren't overheard by a passing trooper, "there's barely enough of them to man the gate and conduct perimeter patrols."

Johnson nodded his thanks once and strode away, back to the room he had come from shortly before.

"Corporal Daniels," he snapped as he walked in, seeing that Mander was already engaged in conversation with an earphone clasped to the left side of his head, "get me assault troop if you will."

Seconds later, following the brief hail and response ritual, assault troop's temporary commander, Sergeant Maxwell, spoke to him.

"Foxtrot-Fiver-Zero-Alpha here, go ahead," Maxwell said,

"It's Foxtrot-Three-Three-Alpha," Johnson said, giving the callsign that identified himself. "I need you to debrief the senior RMP on site and send two Spartans back out to follow the route they give you for the rest of their unit. Report back to me directly when you have something." With that, he stepped away from the controls and walked out, shouting aggressive encouragement for the men to move their arses if they wanted to see their next birthdays.

The rest of the squadron assembled in convoy a little under an hour later under the watchful eye of Squadron Sergeant Major Johnson. The SSM was now adorned with full battle gear and wearing webbing stocked with full magazines for the Sterling submachine gun he hefted, its folding stock locked in the forward position to reduce the size and bulk of the weapon. He looked pointedly at his watch to convey that they were all running the risk of personally disappointing him.

Allowing One Troop to take the lead, he followed in the first of the two Sultan command vehicles behind them, which acted as their mobile headquarters. In turn, behind them snaked nine fully-loaded green Bedford trucks which, combined with the light armour ahead of them and the remaining two troops of Fox APCs behind, made a cacophonous noise of loud diesel engines.

Nodding towards Daniels, who was operating the vehicle in his APC, the radio operator spoke the words of command which set them off on their loud, slow journey towards an area they were to defend and consolidate.

Home soil or not, they were going to war.

"Hello Foxtrot-Three-Three-Alpha, this is Foxtrot-Five-Zero," came Maxwell's voice from the radio again.

Making eye contact with Daniels, Johnson nodded and pressed the button to answer on his headset with attached boom microphone.

"We've located what we believe was the RMP unit, or at least their transport. Over."

"Go on. Over," Johnson said, fearing that the next update might become even less comfortable.

"Sir, we can see signs of a contact; spent casings and some blood, and their Land Rovers are in the ditch. Over," Maxwell said in a flat tone.

Johnson knew Maxwell to be a trustworthy man who had never failed to control his nerves. He led from the front, and this fostered the respect from his men to follow him, as much as it eliminated any need for them to fear him. Now, however, he was clearly unhappy.

"Extend a search pattern for two hundred metres, then report back to base. Out," Johnson told him.

Have a look around, then fuck off out of there, he thought to himself before crinkling his brow in confusion.

Crashed Land Rovers? Spent casings? How had they driven their vehicles off the road and exchanged fire, evidently taking casualties in the process, and not made it back or called for assistance?

Shaking those thoughts off, Johnson kept his eyes on the limited view forward as his tracked vehicle screeched and ground its way forward in convoy. Twenty minutes later, Maxwell called him up again to report that no casualties or survivors could be found within the radius given, and that ammunition and supplies had been abandoned. Thinking for a second and deciding that the Land Rovers were less useful, given that there were many more available, and that he had far better equipped armoured vehicles on site, he ordered half of his assault troop to retrieve the arms and equipment and return to base for their arrival.

That arrival happened after another hour, as the long, snaking convoy rolled through the gates where Maxwell had arrayed his four Spartan APCs. These were lighter, faster tracked vehicles than his own ride, or the far more heavily equipped Fox cars which comprised the majority of their fighting force. Maxwell had his APCs in formation facing the main gate where their belt-fed 7.62 General Purpose Machine Guns, GPMGs or Gympies, could be brought to bear in overlapping arcs of fire. Johnson had the driver of his Sultan pull in just behind his assault troop, and climbed out and down as he watched the remainder of the convoy roll in.

He trusted that Rochefort and Croft would organise that side of things efficiently, allocating the men barracks and finding appropriate space for stores, at the same time as setting up a command post and organising the four troops to rotate on sentry duty.

As much as it pained him to leave the details of his squadron to other people, he forced himself to act as the commander and trust the other NCOs to do what needed to be done. Walking towards the RMP sergeant, he saw the man snap to attention.

That was one of the vagaries of his rank; he was sometimes a 'Sir' to the men, a 'Mister' to the officers, and to younger enlisted men, he was often seen as something near to God himself. He knew that wasn't true, of course, that title was reserved for Regimental Sergeant Majors.

"At ease, Sergeant," he said, accepting the officer treatment from the man, who seemed young for an RMP sergeant in Johnson's eyes. He asked him to repeat the information he had already given to Maxwell.

"Sir, Sergeant Swift. I was left in charge of the garrison when Captain Sinclair and Lieutenant Harrison took the rest of the unit out and didn't return," he said curtly, betraying the slightest trace of annoyance at having to repeat himself again.

"No radio contact?" the man shook his head. "No agreed rendezvous points?" Again, another shake.

Amateurs, Johnson thought unkindly, remembering with a grimace how the regular troops often refused to mix with his reservists, thinking them to be less than real soldiers.

"And you've heard what my men found?" he said, his brain sparking with a mix of fear and pride as he referred to the squadron as 'my men'.

"Yes, Sir," he said, his face a grimace as he forced the emotion away.

"Very well," Johnson said, a little more kindly than before, "stand your men down for now, grab a brew, and come find me later."

With that, he gave the man a gentle slap on the back of one shoulder and watched as he whistled to get the attention of the other red caps, who looked up expectantly as he shouted, "Double in, and I ain't talking about the place in Ireland." His small team jogged to him to follow him back to the gatehouse they occupied. Johnson turned his face back to the gate, where Sergeant Maxwell was gesturing at two squads of four men to conduct a dismounted patrol inside the perimeter, walking in opposing directions and folding out the stocks of their sub-machine guns. The remaining half of his troop, the ones who had found the scene where the RMPs had run into some unknown trouble, were arrayed in front of the gates and manning the four big machine guns.

Nodding to himself in satisfaction, Johnson strode back to his APC and rode the short distance to the main administrative building complex.

Inside, Croft and Rochefort had already set up the command post and were issuing orders for supplies to be unloaded and stored safely. No sooner had he been brought up to speed with things, than Maxwell called up from the front gate.

"Civilians incoming, Staff," Mander said to Rochefort, using the working title for his rank and position. "Sergeant Maxwell is asking for orders."

Rochefort looked to Johnson, who nodded, giving him permission to use his initiative and make decisions.

"Sergeant Croft?" Rochefort shouted as he left the room, no doubt recruiting the admin troop sergeant to give him men and provisions to assist the expected influx of civilians in need of shelter and management.

"Get Maxwell back," Johnson told the radio operator, "and tell him to disarm all civilians at the gate. Issue chitties and ask him to keep a record, but no guns inside the wire. Understood?"

"Understood, Sir," he replied, then called Maxwell's troop on the radio to relay the orders.

Chapter 12

Running flat out, his backpack bumping uncomfortably up and down and the dog flanking him low to the ground, Peter headed straight back to his house as fast as he could move. The scream had been long and loud and had carried over a mile, but the distance did nothing to remove the pain and terror conveyed in the high-pitched shriek.

He had instinctively known that something was terribly wrong, that the scream wasn't him being called back for punishment, and that whatever he was about to face, whatever he was soon to discover would not be good.

That realisation, as much as it dropped his heart through his stomach and gave him a speed and lightness of foot that he had never thought he was capable of, did nothing to assuage the terror he felt when he burst through the trees and crossed the back garden to skid to a stop. He froze in horror, looking at a blood-soaked pile of bodies all slumped on the few steps at the side of the patio area. One of those bodies, marked out as unique by the fact that it was the only one to be moving, let out another ear-piercing shriek of rage and fear and other emotions that his young mind could not interpret.

Stepping closer, his feet moving without conscious effort, he began to discern different things from the pile. A woman with grey skin lay to one side of the main event, the back of her head flattened and leaking a dark, thick substance.

A fat man, his bloated belly exposed by the shirt which had been torn away, lay atop another man. He also had grey skin, but his had been a darker shade to begin with, and he was wearing the same shirt as the woman, like they both worked in the same place.

The fatter man's face was upturned, his dark purple gums exposed to show dirty teeth below one eye. The other, he saw in revulsion, was a mess of gore and had been ruined. A deep score mark ran down the side of the face turned towards him, and the man underneath posthumously told him what had happened. The pitchfork, which had always been propped against the wall just a few paces from where he now stood rooted to the spot, was resting with the wooden shaft of the handle pointing upwards, and the tines of the fork embedded in the face of the last corpse, with a tine through each eye socket.

Bizarrely, his mind taking in the most infinitesimally minor details, he saw that the nearest of the four tines of the fork was disfigured at the tip, most likely caused when it had impacted the concrete with enough force to bend the metal.

As for who had thrust the pitchfork downwards, that was a simple question to answer. His mother, usually so scowling and calculating, looked up at him with pleading eyes. Those eyes belonged to a much younger person than the woman he knew, as though in her fear and grief she had revealed herself to him finally, showing someone just as scared and vulnerable as he was.

Just as he was beginning to feel something bordering on sympathy for her, her mouth twisted into a rictus of anger and her eyes narrowed at him.

"Where were you, you little shit?" she snarled, and struggled to get to her feet as she kept her right hand clamped over her left forearm. "Where did you go, eh?"

"I..." Peter began, conditioned never to make the woman ask him something twice unless he wanted to be slapped.

"What?" she said, sticking out her bottom lip in cruel mockery of his own expression. "Did the wittle baby get scared?"

The tears streaming down her face and the uncontrollable quiver of her chin betrayed her savage and cruel words. She was scared.

Scared, he thought, and from what he saw, hurt too.

She clutched at her left forearm with her right hand, bright red blood pulsing and oozing through her clenched fingers. Her breathing was rapid and shallow, and Peter hesitated a second too long and saw her draw in a breath to snap more insults at him, but instead her breath caught in her throat and she gagged and coughed uncontrollably.

Her eyes looked up at him, half pleading and half in anger which she chose to direct at him for no particular reason other than the fact that he was there. She wriggled out from under the edge of the two dead bodies, which Peter was trying his hardest not to look at, and she struggled to regain her feet.

She fell back down twice until she could reach out a steadying hand, allowing the flow of blood to pour out quicker, and Peter earned a snapshot of the wound just above her wrist.

He could see a flash of white globules of almost mustard yellow jelly below the horribly torn skin and missing flesh. Such an array of different colours and textures in that tiny freeze-frame he had seen of the cross-section in her arm both fascinated and horrified him, but seeing her raise herself to her height, which was barely higher than his own, sobered him, forcing an involuntary step backwards to place him out of arm's reach.

"Help me inside," she gasped, leaning against the rough brick of the house and closing her eyes momentarily.

Peter had seen injuries before, even some bad ones. Growing up on a farm where dangerous machinery operated every day was bound to draw some blood to see, and he had even seen the results of a man foolish enough to try to dislodge packed grass in a heavy-bladed mower with his boot, and he had witnessed first-hand the shock and pain that such a deep wound could invoke.

This, however, seemed eerily different.

Instead of the pain and the shock causing shouts and screams and strings of foul swear words, as he would expect from experience, she seemed horribly subdued and quiet. For a woman who never missed an opportunity to belittle or berate him, the fact that she seemed so cowed by what was effectively a large cut to her arm worried him.

He did as he was told and helped her the half dozen paces to the rear door to the house, as he still tried not to look at the small pile of dead meat that used to be people. It was an ever-increasingly difficult struggle as she seemed to weaken with each step, but he eventually got her back to her preferred spot, where she could prioritise her affairs.

Struggling to open the lid of the bottle with her blood-slicked hands, she wordlessly thrust it in his direction and watched him expectantly as he used the hem of his t-shirt to clean the sticky, dark red mess from the neck and open it. She snatched it weakly from him and slumped backwards to tip the bottle lazily up to her mouth and close her eyes.

Taking the initiative, he went to the kitchen and pulled out a wooden chair from the table, which he carefully stood on to reach the dusty section above one of the kitchen cabinets to retrieve the battered tin which served as their first aid kit. Blinking away the dust in his eyes as he carefully climbed back down and sifted through the old contents, he selected a paper packet containing a gauze pad and a rolled bandage which had been white at one point in its existence. Returning to her, he saw her right hand fluttering weakly as she tried to open the cigarette packet with one hand by propping it against her thigh. He reached out tentatively, taking the pack from her unresisting hands and carefully took one out to offer it to her, filter first. Her eyes, as dark and glazed-over as they were, still registered a flicker of her dislike for him, but didn't burn with the intensity she usually seemed to feel.

Taking the cigarette in her lips and keeping her eyes on him, she watched as he picked up the lighter and rolled his thumb over the flint wheel to land on the gas switch. The action was unfamiliar and slightly alien to him, but he managed to spark a flame on his third attempt, and he held it out gingerly towards the tip of the cigarette as it shook visibly to complement her actions. Sucking greedily on the small white stick, the tiny flame was pulled towards the end, which glowed orange in sudden response to the contact with the small, man-made fire. Releasing his thumb, Peter blinked suddenly in response to the stream of smoke she blew out straight ahead of her and into his face.

He knelt down and shuffled closer to her, holding out the dressing and bandage, seeking silent permission to come near her. She closed her eyes, giving no indication that he shouldn't continue, and the only sign that she was alive was a shallow, rhythmic breathing which was interspersed at irregular intervals by her pausing to take long pulls on the cigarette which hung from her dry lips. Reaching out, he carefully placed the gauze pad over the torn flesh on her forearm, then warily wrapped the bandage around it.

"Tighter than that…" she mumbled past her smoke, without opening her eyes.

Her words were barely understandable, but he knew enough not to ignore her commands. Pulling on the slightly stretchy material of the bandage he felt her body stiffen with the increased pain and wrapped the rest around the injury until no blood leaked through.

Unsure if she was still conscious, as she hadn't moved for a few seconds after he had finished, Peter held his breath until he saw the tip of the cigarette glow red and lift up slightly. Standing up, he paused as a sensation grabbed his attention momentarily. Freezing where he was, he tried to understand what instinct had pricked at him until he realised it was heat; heat from her, radiating outwards like a fire. Reaching for her forehead as he had seen adults do to children who claimed to be feeling ill, he paused, fearful for a brief second that she would take offence at him being close enough to touch her, then decided – hoped - that she wouldn't be able to hit him in her state.

Her forehead was uncomfortably hot to touch, and her skin felt sweaty in parts and dry in others, as though the moisture leaking through her pores had burned away like drops of water on the concrete slabs of their patio in summer. She writhed slightly, her lower lip shivering in time with her chin as her shallow gasps for breath tried to form words.

He considered finding a blanket to cover her as he had seen actors on television do with people who were hurt or unwell, but seeing as the heat emanating from her felt like it was growing in intensity, he stepped backwards as she dropped into a sleep-like state and burned up. Peter turned and went to shut the back door he had left open.

Hovering half out of the doorway, his gaze fell on the pile of bodies and fixed on the pitchfork buried in the skull of the man who, judging by the fresh red blood still wet on his teeth, had been the one to bite his mother.

Smiling slightly despite the fear and horror of the sudden turn of events, he closed and locked the door.

~

As the sun set that evening, Squadron Sergeant Major Johnson toured the camp and checked in with all five of his combined troops. Two Troop were now guarding the gate and checking in the steady stream of civilian refugees who had dutifully arrived after the cryptic phone calls from their army reservist family members.

None who arrived knew what was happening in the wider world, but one or two had seen bizarre happenings which they had sensibly stayed clear of.

"One chap smashed through the downstairs window of a house," said a woman who had clearly dressed for the occasion with her best coat and gloves over a dress which seemed a little too summery for the chill days of early spring. "He was covered from head to toe in blood. He must have been very angry, or probably on drugs," she opined haughtily as she stared at Johnson for an appropriate response.

"Yes, madam," he said as he cracked a small smile which was entirely obscured by his large moustache, "now, if you wouldn't mind signing in with the others?"

He walked away before she could protest, and he suspected that she would probably complain about the standard of accommodation on offer. Allowing himself a cruel smirk, he tried to imagine what her face would look like after she had received Sergeant Croft's hastily organised induction lecture, which all civilian arrivals had been subjected to. It did not mince words or sugar coat anything; it told the cold, hard facts as they were known, and it served to instil in their minds their total reliance on the military personnel for their safety and protection. That way, whatever orders they were given were more likely to be followed precisely and in a timely fashion.

Welcome to the Green Machine, folks. Johnson thought to himself with glee. *Hurry up and wait, stand in line, and follow the process.*

Whilst his mind made jokes, a deeper, darker level of his subconscious harboured a growing sense of doom. It nurtured and fed it, as though his mind had found a dangerous animal not long after birth and was now too scared to walk into the shed where it had grown into a killer. That feeling, as much as he tried to repress it, found a sudden route for expressing itself not an hour later, just as the sun began to set.

One of the people forming the steady flow of human traffic heading for their well-guarded gate was running and out of breath, waving his arms at the soldiers and yelling from a distance where they could not hear his words.

Johnson, not far from the gate and talking to one of the troop Corporals on gate sentry duty, heard the commotion; not the shouts, but orders being given calmly, and the sound of turrets traversing on two of the APCs watching the entrance to line up the devastating power of the 30mm canon and the 7.62 co-axial machine gun on the source of the disruption.

Johnson unslung the Sterling sub-machine gun from over his right shoulder and stalked towards the gate where the shouted voices began to take form in his ears.

"Behind me…" shouted the man running awkwardly towards the nearest tree cover which was still some distance away, "…tried to bite me…"

"Sergeant?" snapped Johnson at the RMP and his Corporal who had returned to the gate for a lack of anything worthwhile to do, as he pointed forwards at the man. Johnson was suddenly performing at a heightened state of attention thanks to the dump of adrenaline hitting his body. "Secure that man and lock the gates afterwards," he added.

"Gunners," he called in a raised voice, "track target but do not fire unless ordered."

He didn't wait for an acknowledgement, but strode forward to watch as the hysterical man was ordered to his knees and searched before having his hands bound behind him. He said a very brief but silent prayer of thanks that the red caps were there, as prisoner handling was one of their dedicated roles which his own cavalrymen weren't trained for.

Johnson watched as the man stared down the entire length of the Military Policeman's heavy 7.62 Self Loading Rifle, as this silenced him and seemed to focus his attention towards understanding every command he was given and following them to the letter.

Johnson scanned the ground ahead, seeing nothing. "Call out when you see something," he shouted to the men within earshot, earning an almost immediate response as a trooper, peering out of the open hatch of one of the Fox armoured cars with binoculars to his face, shouted his rank.

"Talk to me," Johnson responded in a loud growl.

"Two o-clock, partially obscured by low ground and tall grass, three hundred yards," said the trooper in a young but clear voice. "One person, male I think."

That seemed to be the entire threat report. No mention of weapons or other people. Something the man, who now lay face down as his bound hands were lifted up for him to be searched, had said now scratched at the inside of Johnson's skull.

"...*tried to bite me,*" he had said. Seconds ticked by in strained silence as the trooper called out a very slow progress report on the movement of their only contact.

"Clear this gate of non-essential personnel," Johnson barked, sensing more than hearing the sound of boots scraping as at least two men responded to his orders.

He watched intently, now able to see the outline of the approaching man, with the sun beginning to set somewhere far behind his left shoulder, and he knew instantly that something was very wrong about the slowly-encroaching threat. He had to wait a full three minutes as he endured the agonisingly slow updates from the trooper with the binoculars, until the SSM's nerve broke and he climbed up to the front of the big armoured car and held his hand out for the instrument. Placing the glasses to his eyes, he fought to control the gasp threatening to escape his throat. Something flapped under the man's face, as though a purse swung from his mouth and lolled grotesquely with the jerky movements of his footfalls. Twice he saw the man fall, only to slowly regain his feet and stumble onwards.

Eventually, progressing at an excruciatingly slow pace, Johnson no longer needed the binoculars to see the man, and what was much worse was the realisation that the thing swinging from under the man's head, was his lower jaw held tenuously on one side by flesh and sinew.

"Christ on a fucking bike," Johnson muttered under his breath, swallowing to calm his roiling stomach.

Chapter 13

"Hold your fire," Johnson said in a voice that invited no disobedience. He lowered his own weapon and wandered towards the man, or the *thing* that had been, up until recently, a man. It stumbled headlong into the fence, rebounded, then tried again to bull its way through the seemingly invisible force field that was reinforced chain link. Johnson, feeling secure behind the fence with a two-foot buffer of space between them, stepped close enough to see and smell the man.

The smell was what caught his attention first, because it smelt like old meat and shit. The latter because the man had clearly soiled himself, but the former puzzled the soldier. When the acrid smell had pricked at his eyeballs and prompted a responding drop of water to form in both eyes, Johnson took an exaggerated step back and was startled into taking a second when the man without a full face snapped his head towards him and snarled, throwing himself against the fence once more with increased excitement.

Johnson was locked into its gaze then, his own brown eyes mirroring the milky orbs that stared back at him. The thing looked like it had cataracts and would surely be blind and unable to focus through the cloudy vision, but somehow it zeroed in on him effortlessly, and held the acquired target like a hawk looking down on prey.

The soldier slowly took a long step to his right, away from the gatehouse, and the thing followed his movement like a stumbling, rotten mirror image.

He, *it*, was wearing a torn shirt which had once been pale yellow, and light brown trousers. One dark tan shoe remained affixed to one foot, the other lost somewhere nobody knew. The breathing, if the noises it made could be called breathing, came in whistling hisses in and out and made different noises as it did so, like an old set of bellows.

He tilted his head, locked into its terrifying visage and unable to look away, and the thing mirrored his slow movements like some awful reflection from the other side of a horrible death.

"Sir, permission to engage?" came a shaky voice from behind his left shoulder. In response to the new sound, the thing snapped its head right and homed in on the source of the interruption as though this new thing consumed the entire attention span of the mangled man. The hissing, groaning, rattling noise that emanated from the mouth, or half of the mouth to be precise, of the thing before Johnson ramped up by a factor of five as it threw itself once more into the chain link. This time, as it tried to force its face through the too-small gaps in the metal, the side of its lower jaw that still clung on to the upper half snagged in the fence and stuck.

Horrified, Johnson swallowed the spasm in his gullet that threatened to bring up the last cup of tea and biscuit he had thrown down his neck, just as the thing pulled away and he watched in gory, seemingly slow-motion detail as the remaining skin tore and stretched to its limit, before the resistance finally became too much and the jawbone dropped to land on the soft grass with a gentle thump.

It was too much for the trooper who had approached behind his left flank, and he dropped to his knees as he vomited uncontrollably.

Something, either the sound of the retching or the smell of the regurgitated food or both, whipped the now chinless man into a desperate frenzy, and a new sound ripped from him.

"Eeeeeeeeerrrrrrrgh," it screeched on an inward breath, making a sound that was the direct fleshy equivalent of nails being dragged down a chalkboard. It seemed to vibrate as it threw itself over and over into the chain link fence again and again, until the force of meat hitting metal rang an echoing sound along their section of the perimeter and threatened to bring yet more unwanted attention to them. Thinking, Johnson cast his eyes around the grass at his feet and located a raised tuft of thicker, more hard-wearing grass. Using the heel of his boot like a pickaxe, he swung a few times until the clump came loose, then reached down to grasp the stalks and heave the lump of turf high over the fence and away, behind the thing as though he were tossing the severed head of an enemy by its hair.

As soon as that thought came to him, before the replacement for a severed head landed, he admonished himself for having the idea and drawing the similarity.

When the grass did land, the soft thud made the screeching noise stop, and he watched in stunned silence as the thing temporarily lost all interest in the trooper, who was still throwing up the remainder of his last meal, as well as the SSM who he had been so feverishly trying to get to before the interruption. The thing staggered away in the direction of the last noise. No sooner had it stumbled five paces away than Johnson cleared his throat and made it spin its head back towards him, and it reached out in the direction of the latest sound which had caught its attention.

Not bothering to fold out the stock of the gun, he raised it and fired a short burst into the chest of the man at a range of about four paces. Convulsing like a landed fish, the man was thrown bodily backwards to hit the earth flat on his back. Johnson reapplied the safety on his gun and lowered the barrel just as he froze and dropped his jaw. The man, a handful of bullets riddling his chest, began to hiss and moan again, although in a different tone due to the holes in his lungs. Haltingly, it dragged itself upright and back to its feet to reach out towards him with both hands.

Interesting, he thought to himself, as he calmly drew the eight-inch bayonet and slowly twisted it onto the end of the lightened barrel of his sub-machine gun. He had rarely seen bayonets in his career, but had long since given up wondering where Rochefort had found the random and unexpected boxes of forgotten gems.

Settling the blade into place and feeling the satisfying click as it locked in position at the diagonal angle to the magazine sticking horizontally out of the opposite side of the gun, he took two swift paces forwards and raised the gun to drive the bayonet straight through the open maw to burst the very tip of the blade out of the back of the skull. The man, the *thing*, became instantly lifeless, and as Johnson withdrew the blade as though demonstrating perfect form to raw recruits, he watched as his victim crumpled to the ground at his feet on the other side of the fence. He removed the blade from the weapon and wiped it delicately on the grass before restoring it to the leather sheath and turning.

"On your feet, Trooper," he said to the shocked young man, who probably hadn't breathed since he had finished throwing up, "and get that bloody beret off your eyes; it's not a cap." Then he strode purposefully towards the buildings as he fought the urge to fall to his own knees and burst into hysterical tears of crippling fear. Recalling the words that the naval air base to their north east had reported to them, his whole body went cold in shock and fear as the line returned to him once again with renewed meaning.

The dead were rising.

~

Miles away, sitting alone in the gathering dark and growing fear, Peter watched.

He watched from the seat that his father used to occupy as his mother remained unchanged for hours.

She breathed fast, the sounds eventually transforming into shallow gasps as she snatched the oxygen from the air with ever-increasing desperation. Just after she had lost consciousness, Peter had tried the telephone and waited for painful seconds as the dial clicked all the way back from the three consecutive nines he had dialled. He didn't understand the tone, but the line didn't connect to anything at the other end. He tried twice more, each time failing to get through to anyone.

By the time her breathing began to slow to the sporadic gasps which rattled from her throat, Peter could feel the heat radiating away from her red-hot skin. He knew that she wasn't going to get better, not that he could explain why or how he felt that way, just that he knew and accepted it on a level of pure belief. As that realisation settled on his soul, and he recognised that it didn't trouble him, he rose from the seat and went to fetch himself some food from the kitchen.

Peter had no way of knowing the complex biological processes that had taken place inside his mother's body, nor would he have fully understood them even if they were explained in a fashion more suited to the learning capacity of a nine-year-old boy.

He would not have known that her body temperature had risen to above forty-four degrees Celsius, and that the rampant fever that was destroying her from within had effectively boiled her brain and damaged it beyond all salvageable levels. She had lost all higher brain function and was left with that part of her mind which was purely instinctive and uncontrollable; the part that remembered to breathe when she was asleep, or that reminded her heart to beat without any conscious thought. That part of her, so deeply buried by years of social evolution, by generations upon generations of civilised tweaks to the genetic code of her race, *that* still knew how to hunt and kill for food even if *she* didn't know it.

Human beings are carnivores. Their eyes are forward-facing to better locate prey and gauge distance. They have incisors and canine teeth designed for killing other animals and ripping flesh. Humans might have forgotten these facts, but their deeply suppressed brain functions had not.

Just as the fever finally killed her body, the virus that had infected her when the saliva of the man who had bitten her came into contact with her blood and torn-open flesh took over. It kept certain aspects of her body alive but retained none of what made her the person she was.

Had Peter known this, it was doubtful that he would really have cared, because he hated the person she was.

He hated her on such a deep, cellular level that he might as well have been infected with something just as virulent and potent as the disease which killed her, as he stood in the next room and ate a sandwich without using a plate, not caring if the crumbs falling to the floor would result in him being hit or shouted at.

Just as he finally began to accept that his life was never going to go back to normal, he heard a snarling, ripping, yelping sound from the other room.

Freezing in mid-chew, the half a sandwich still hovering near to his mouth, the sickening sounds of butchery drifted through the downstairs of the house to his ears. Unmoving for longer than he could possibly be aware of, he began to breathe again. His breath didn't come in panicked gasps, because he too had unlocked some deep, primal ability which he didn't know he possessed.

Peter, unknowingly, was a born survivor.

Keeping his breathing soft and quiet, he moved off the kitchen side and crept forwards in a half crouch as he placed one foot carefully after the other to cross the small yet impossibly long distance to the doorway, in his attempt to add vision to the sounds he could hear.

Rounding the doorway with just one eye and a tiny portion of his face, he couldn't contain himself any longer and almost let out a cry of horror. On the other side of the room, down on the floor on her knees, was his mother.

Her hands ripped at the blood-soaked mess of fur and meat and organs which she was pulling apart hungrily.

As disciplined as Peter was by keeping silent, he could not control what his bladder did involuntarily as it emptied to run down his right leg. Before the hot liquid had reached the rough, brown carpet, his mother froze and stopped ripping at the corpse of their dog. She lifted her head up in the air and sniffed; long, hungry pulls through her nostrils as she tried to locate the source of the acrid smell of ammonia.

Spinning her head faster than he had ever seen her move, she whipped around to face him, apparently having forgotten all about the dog she had been tearing apart with her teeth and her nails.

Unfreezing from the spot as rapidly as he had become stuck there in the first place, Peter turned and fled. Skidding on the kitchen linoleum as his right foot was wet with urine, he slammed into the floor to scramble upright and fly towards the back door, where he snatched up his backpack without breaking step. Spilling from the door, he slammed it behind him just in time, as she was pressed against the pane of glass as though she were trying to chew her way through it.

Standing there, just inches from the woman who had enjoyed hurting him every day of his life that he could recall, he felt no change in his attitude towards her, even now that she seemed to be a wild animal and a murderer.

Backing away as he slipped his arms into the straps of his bag, his left foot bumped the outstretched hand of the dead fat man and made him stumble but not fall. Turning away, he made straight for the gap in the trees, and vanished into the gathering dark.

Chapter 14

Peter shivered through the night, partly because of the chill air cooling the wet trouser leg he'd had to endure, but mostly through shock and fear. He had found himself somewhere high and relatively sheltered to spend the night in the upper floor of the barn, but that was still fairly exposed to the gentle wind that blew between the prefabricated panels, and it had forced him to stack some hay bales to provide a wind break.

He had fled wearing only a thin sweatshirt, but finding a thick, black coat of heavy, close-knit wool had been heavenly. Wrapped up inside the stiff, oversized garment which his father had called a donkey jacket, he settled down and tried to find sleep.

But sleep would not come, and every time he closed his eyes to turn the murky grey of the moonlit night into the black behind his eyelids, the scene of the dog torn to pieces and his mother ripping and chewing at it flashed vividly in his mind's eye. He replayed the scene from colourful memory over and over like a short film stuck on loop, and it seemed to him that every time he saw it, he was drawn into his mother's cloudy eyes deeper and deeper, until he felt as though she had pulled him close enough for her bloodstained teeth to bite down on his thin arm and tear out a chunk of flesh, just as had happened to her.

He had never seen a zombie film. Never read a book about the dead reanimating or seen comics or anything like it. The word itself – zombie – was barely ever used, because its relevance in normal society was unrecognised in most places. All he knew, and with a child's perspective that made the facts all the more intense, was that his mother had been bitten by a person, then she had burned a fever, then she had woken up and torn the dog to pieces and eaten it. She would have eaten him, too, but he had got away.

Trying to work it through logically, he relayed the facts of the last few days over and over until it no longer made a semblance of sense, but instead confused him worse than before he had started trying to understand. Telling himself to keep to the facts, he laid out the world as he now knew it.

He was on his own.

People bit other people, then they got whatever it was.

People who had been bitten tried to eat you.

One other fact left off his list tickled at the very fringe of being an idea. As he concentrated more, shutting out the wind and the cold and the fear, he connected the dots.

When they are Biters, he thought, making up the name on the spot, given their most prevalent behaviour, *they die if you stab them in the head.*

That thought stayed with him more than the other facts as he drifted in and out of restless slumber throughout the rest of the night.

When he woke, the sky was still the steely-grey pre-dawn with just the slightest of hints of a horizontal slice of yellowy orange in the distance. He knew he wouldn't be able to sleep any longer, and he decided that he had enough light to return home and do what he knew had to be done. Climbing down and sitting at a hay bale at ground level as he ate Nik Naks and a Mars bar for breakfast, he left the heavy jacket over his backpack of goodies and straightened his resolve as he aimed for his house.

Finding the scene at the back door unchanged, barring the absence of his mother gnawing at the glass and squashing her face to smear frothing blood over the single pane, he took three deep breaths as he maintained an awareness of his surroundings. Three people, no three *Biters,* had wandered up to their house, and they lived in the middle of nowhere, so there was no way to be certain that he was safe just because there weren't usually any people around. He cleared his throat for the purpose of clearing his throat, and not to gain anyone's attention, and reached out for the pitchfork which still stood almost upright as it was buried in the unmoving skull where it had been so forcefully placed.

Tugging with both hands to free it, he staggered backwards as it came loose in some grotesque parody of the animated film he had watched so many times with his sister. It had been one of the only VHS cassettes specifically for them in the house, so their choice of things to watch when they were left alone was limited. Still, he imagined himself becoming the king of all the land when the old pitchfork came free, and he held it aloft just as he had seen the character do in the film.

Nothing happened. No ray of light burst from the heavens to shine down on him and no music blasted from unseen speakers to announce his presence to the world.

Instead, a loud noise startled him as his mother banged her face into the glass again to try and chew her way out to kill him, smearing the pane with dark gore. Lowering the pitchfork and spinning the wooden handle in both hands in physical preparation for the act that he had mentally practised throughout the night, he rolled his shoulders and, for the first time in his life, got ready to stand up for himself against his mother.

Stepping forwards and snatching down the back door handle, he stepped smartly back as she screeched loudly, as if they were both psyching themselves up for the confrontation. Then she spilled out of the doorway and fell headfirst down the raised step, to slap noisily on her front at his feet. Stepping backwards slowly as though magnetised into keeping a certain distance, like he was physically repelled by her, he watched her halting, inhuman movements.

She moved her arms, one by one, slowly as though her short fall had dazed her, then raised her head and reached out to him with one hand as she hissed inwards with an accompanying groan; the dried blood of her last meal dark and crusted as it flaked off her face and hands.

Peter stepped back with one foot to steady himself, raised the pitchfork with both hands and angled the curved metal tines as best he could estimate, then struck as he stamped his left foot forward and buried a single spike through her eye socket to grate the end sickeningly against the inside of her skull. She froze, twitched three times with lessening intensity, then slumped forwards as he withdrew the metal.

Looking down at the now lifeless form that used to be his mother, Peter spoke softly.

"That was for nothing," he said, with resounding finality and not a single trace of remorse, "and there's plenty more where that came from."

~

"Right, you tossers!" Squadron Sergeant Major Johnson bawled as he strode into the room where the majority of his troopers were sleeping, "hands off cocks and grab socks."

He had roused them just before dawn, having woken over an hour before to shave and dress in his uniform. He wasn't just the man in charge of the squadron, he was also its heart and soul. Its mascot and talisman.

The RMP unit had volunteered to take the night duty, which Johnson had readily agreed to, but insisted that Three Troop remain on standby to act as the quick reaction force should the RMPs meet any threat that could not be avoided or easily tackled by their reduced numbers.

Following the incident which had threatened to rob him of his wits, not to mention control of his suddenly liquid bowels, he had issued standing orders to the entire squadron, which had apparently now absorbed the eight red caps left behind as the detritus of an unexpected conflict. Those orders were based on the few pieces of valuable information he had gleaned during his brief period of intimacy with one of the things.

The Screechers, as he had called them, given the most penetrative sound the thing had made, a noise that had stayed buried deep in his mind, did not die through conventional means. He had proven that with the half a dozen bullets he had stitched through the chest of the thing at very close range.

Headshots, he had warned, or a bayonet to the brain preferably, given their very highly attuned aural acuity. A hand had gone up at that point.

"Yes," he said in a tired tone that already bordered dangerously on annoyance, "Trooper Nevin?"

"Sir, what's aural acuity mean?" asked Paul Nevin, a man of sufficient age and with enough service to have been a full corporal at least, but in possession of a perpetual laziness and poor attitude.

"It means, Trooper," Johnson said in a tone riddled with warning, "that the things do hear very good and probably better than what you do…" he trailed off after delivering the offensive retort in a voice that told everyone listening precisely what he thought about the mental capacity of Trooper Nevin. His biggest challenge was reading the Sun's page three; that was when he could look beyond Samantha Fox to see the words. Johnson's stare lingered for a few more uncomfortable seconds on the man who he was certain had interrupted him for the sake of having an audience, as opposed to genuinely not knowing the correct terminology for sharp hearing. Uncomfortable seconds for Nevin at least, before he resumed his briefing.

Headshots, or bayonets if they could keep it quiet, were the order of business. Strict discipline regarding noise was to be enforced, and all NCOs were directly responsible for maintaining that discipline.

"As for today," Johnson went on in his loud, powerful voice, "Two and Three Troops will remain here with Admin troop under the command of the SQMS. Our RMP brethren will be standing down for the daytime after the rest of us leave. One Troop and Assault will be on patrol with me." He looked at his watch, "Oh-seven-hundred we are off, so be ready, and one last thing…" he said loudly as he glowered at the assembled men, "We will not observe the normal practice involving RMPs on gate sentry and eggs. Am I clear?"

Mumbles of an affirmative nature and downward-cast eyes gave him as much answer as he would get without singling any one man out, but he had made his point.

"And me, Mister Johnson? Where might I best serve the squadron?" asked a nasal voice which was quickly followed by what Johnson could only describe as a smell like a tart's handbag. He turned to see a splendidly uniformed, and sickeningly perfumed, Second Lieutenant Palmer, who had clearly taken his combat uniform to the family tailor in order to achieve the best fit. Johnson's trained eye, however, noted the well-maintained weapon and a healthy supply of additional ammunition.

"Lieutenant Palmer," Johnson said, "you will be in the second Sultan behind me."

Palmer nodded with a hand pressed flat on his chest in an almost mocking gesture of obedience, before he straightened and slipped a thin cigarette into his mouth and lit it as he turned away.

"Where I can keep a fucking eye on you, you bloody dimwit," Johnson added quietly to himself.

Thirty-nine minutes later, with assault troop leading the way with four Spartans in the front, two Sultans in the middle and the un-tracked four-wheeled Fox armoured cars of One Troop behind, Johnson led his small fighting unit out into the picturesque countryside.

They had travelled less than two miles before they met oncoming vehicles, each containing family members with all of their belongings and pets. Each one was flagged down by the leading vehicle and directed straight to the gate, where they were told to be ready to be searched and relieved of any weapons.

Johnson, from his elevated perspective, standing tall out of the open hatch of the armoured vehicle, fancied that these early morning arrivals were the more sensible ones; those who had taken the night to pack and ensure that they had everything they needed. The influx had been steady, and the other senior sergeants had done a good job in telling them how things were, and thus keeping their problems from becoming Johnson's problems.

Now, approaching the nearest town, the full extent of their problems was about to become clear.

~

Peter couldn't stay in that house. The only home he had ever lived in no longer felt like a safe place, nor did he feel any positive emotional attachment to the building. It stank of death, for one thing. The rotting, butcher's shop stench was thick and cloying in his throat, and he couldn't bear to look at the ravaged remains of the dog that had so overtly disliked him, but still was an innocent animal which had been physically ripped apart and died horribly.

He stripped his clothes, and washed with cold water as there was no hot left now that nobody was alive to flick the switch and activate the immersion heater controls. Cold water didn't bother him, as his discomfort at feeling cold seemed to have vanished during that long night he had spent in the windy barn. He seemed to have aged overnight, matured by the indescribably savage turn of events over the last week.

He had lost his sister; his shield against the harsh realities of his parents' lives.

He had lost his father soon afterwards, not that he knew what his fate had been, but he doubted he would have chosen not to come back; he had left his gun and his dog behind, and Peter thought he would value those two things more than his wife or son.

He had lost his mother. Well, he had killed her but that didn't seem to count as a crime because she had already killed three other people and then turned into the same as them, before killing the dog.

And besides, he told himself as though he needed any more justification, *I had to kill her because she was going to eat me, like she did the dog.*

He did wonder how difficult that final rebellious act would have been had he actually enjoyed his life or felt any connection other than mutual hatred for the woman who abused him, but he put that thought aside as an irrelevant one. As young as he was, as inexperienced in life as he felt, he accepted this new reality on a deep level that could not be explained.

This, his subconscious told him, was just how life was now.

Selecting clothes, food and other supplies, he carried his heavy load downstairs and paused by the lounge door. He didn't cast his eyes left because he doubted he could hold his nerve if he saw the ravaged and destroyed body of the dog, so instead he reached out and felt for the door handle as he tried not to breathe in the smell of death. As the door clicked shut, his eyes rested on the hallway cupboard, and he quickly weighed up the risks of doing what he was planning on doing and decided that there was nobody left to punish him. Opening the door and reaching inside, he picked up the heavy shotgun with its long barrels and stooped awkwardly to retrieve the belt, complete with its fully stuffed loops, each one bearing a red plastic tube with a brass cap. Hefting the gun and leaning to one side to lift the cartridge belt over his shoulder, he walked to the kitchen where he put everything down and emptied the cupboard of the food.

Quickly realising that he had more than he could carry, he furrowed his brow in thought for a few seconds before an idea struck him. Turning for the back door and lifting up the pitchfork which would now go with him everywhere, he slipped outside with alert eyes and returned shortly afterwards pulling a four-wheeled cart with a squeaking wheel bearing. Taking it past the house and down the few steps with difficulty, as he had to manoeuvre around the now four dead bodies, he kept his eyes fixed on anything except the corpses.

He took a selection of tools from the shed and added them to the cart, then manhandled it with much more exertion back to the house, where he ferried his bags of clothes and food out to fill the only transport he had available to him.

Turning his back on the house after he closed the back door, he paused, glancing for the first time at the decaying bodies, and feeling the swell of fear rising from his churning stomach again, he considered whether to set fire to the house and destroy the evidence of his childhood and its bloody end. Deciding against the arson, no matter how satisfying it would have been, he dropped the final item onto the top of his haul.

Settling the stuffed lamb in the top of his battered backpack to make it more comfortable, he tightened the zip to keep it safe, and headed for the farm.

Chapter 15

"Stop, stop, stop," Johnson's radio operator called to the armoured column after his hand gesture indicated his orders.

"Signal Assault troop," he shouted to the trooper on the radio, "half of them are to dismount and recce the obstruction. Defile drill."

The man nodded and relayed the orders. Johnson watched as two of the crew dismounted from their tracked wagons, wearing webbing and helmets and carrying their personal weapons. Then they set off forward on foot with the heavy machine guns of the other two serving as cover. If he had ordered the entire troop to dismount, they would have removed the GPMGs, the 7.62mm general purpose machine guns, from their tracked vehicles and taken them along to provide a devastating capability of man-portable weaponry. But Johnson wanted this done quickly, and he wanted his boys back inside the safety of their armoured vehicles as fast as humanly possible.

He was yet to see a set of teeth that could bite through the thick aluminium of their wagons.

Despite his crisp appearance, he had barely slept during the night as he had pored over all of the details he knew, as well as those he was making educated guesses about. One thing that he couldn't yet be sure about was how the, *whatever it was*, infected people. How the dead arose and started acting like the one he had spent quality time with at the fence.

The only way, he decided, was when they bit someone. Just like rabies.

Switching his attention back to the scene ahead, he took a deep breath and watched his boys work. He knew they knew what to do and certainly didn't need him watching over them or holding their hands. As much as he wanted to be at the tip of the spear, he recognised that the need for oversight was more important to the squadron than having their oldest, albeit probably toughest, soldier at the front. And he knew it would serve little purpose other than to assuage his feelings of itchy feet.

He watched on as the eight men leapfrogged each other, as if he were overseeing a training exercise; only he hoped that their eyes would be far more alert than if they were just training. The obstruction that they sent to clear was a cluster of crashed cars. Defile drill was what they did all the time, as the majority of their work was to patrol the areas where it was unsafe to be walking around. Defile drill allowed for an obstruction to be checked for roadside bombs and other dangers, whilst the rest of the troop could bring to bear the full might of their vehicles' weapons. Johnson was running this by the book, and his boys were performing just how they were supposed to.

And that was just it. They were doing exactly what was expected of them in warfare.

Only this wasn't warfare. This was something else entirely.

"Trooper, recall the men," he snapped at his radio operator.

"Sir?" he answered, his voice rising half an octave to betray his lack of experience and youth.

"Do it now," Johnson said, fighting down the sudden anger he felt at having to repeat himself to a green boy. To his credit, the trooper offered no further opportunity to have his head removed by the squadron commander, and gave the orders. No sooner had he overcome one person double-checking his decisions than the radio sparked to life and Lieutenant Palmer's shrill voice cut the air through Johnson's headphones.

"Sergeant Major," his unhurried voice said, seeming to have a direct connection to Johnson's eyebrows until he managed to control his face, "is there a problem?"

Johnson made eye contact with the radio operator and made a cutting motion with his left hand past his throat. The trooper understood.

"Standby, Sir," he said formally.

Johnson returned his gaze to the front, as the eight soldiers jogged back to their armour and climbed inside. Transmitting to the whole group himself, he called out their new orders.

"All troops, Green Snake, I repeat, Green Snake unless otherwise instructed. All troops acknowledge."

He waited as the few acknowledgements came back, satisfied that he had made the right decision. Just as the acknowledgements had finished, assault troop reported that they were ready to move, so he gave the order.

Green Snake meant that instead of approaching any potential threat area or obstruction carefully and dismounting to check for dangers, they were now under orders to force their way through and not stop or leave the safety of their vehicles. He cursed himself in his head that he hadn't thought to abandon conventional protocols when their world had apparently abandoned the conventional overnight. Now, powering through the crashed and abandoned cars blocking their way with their far heavier mounts and more powerful engines, they approached the outskirts of the big town where the county hospital lay just off the main road.

Peeling away from the wider carriageways, Johnson's decision to switch tactics was instantly rewarded. The lead Spartan turned slightly towards the nearside hedge to bump an abandoned Ford Escort off the road and provide clear sight and movement for the remaining vehicles, and just as the upturned front edge of their wedge-shaped tracked vehicle made contact, so did the hedgerow come alive. Johnson counted five, six, then a dozen people who moved just like the one he had seen at the fence at their camp the previous day. Each face that his mind took a mental snap-shot of registered something different from the last; exposed teeth through a ragged hole torn in a cheek, a face masked in blood from a badly torn scalp, a missing arm just above the elbow.

The only two things they had in common were their milky, soulless eyes and their evident intent on getting to the troopers.

"Close down, close down, close down!" Johnson barked into the radio, then dropped his body vertically downwards to lift the heavy, circular hatch lid closed above his head. Their views would be limited now to the thin strips which they had trained to use for so many hours and days. It did not hamper their ability to perform their tasks and carry out their orders. In fact, it made it easier to carry out those orders, as the drivers sealed inside their armour and masked under the noise of their roaring engines couldn't hear the squelches and popping crunches of bodies going under their tracks. They couldn't see this happening, given that their viewports offered a restricted view directly before their wagons, but the feedback from the controls told the story well enough.

Johnson's own vehicle, one of their two Sultan mobile command cars, was effectively the same platform as the Spartans of the assault troop, only his had more room inside to accommodate the large map wall and additional radio operator who relayed his orders. Raising his own seat and opening his hatch again, he took up a firing position with the armaments for the vehicle, the single belt-fed GMPG, and lined up the sights on the approaching bodies as they stumbled into view. He alone of all the armoured column was outside of a sealed reconnaissance tank, as the Fox and Spartan cars could operate their guns from inside, unlike his vehicle, which basically had it mounted on the pintle outside.

His vision of these new enemies was jolting and fleeting at times, but each small visual clue left him with a growing sense of dread and revulsion. New flashes of horrific and bloody injuries seared his eyeballs as his mind lost valuable thinking capacity through imagining how those wounds could have been inflicted. His reverie was snapped back to the present by a request from the rear-most car to open fire on the Screechers.

"Tell him no," Johnson said loudly to the radio operator. "Save the ammo."

As they pushed deeper into the outskirts of the town, the pillar of black smoke became more and more visible from the direction of the hospital, which sat atop a small rise. Calling out the change of destination for it to be relayed, he steered his column away from that area and towards the centre of the town. Pushing slowly through the tighter streets, and nudging cars and vans clear of the road every few hundred yards, their progress had slowed through a combination of shorter sight ranges and more obstructions than there had been on the wider roads outside of the built-up area.

Realising his mistake, Johnson called a full stop and ordered them all to cut their engines.

Sitting near to the main square of the town, its origins going back hundreds and hundreds of years to a time when the town walls kept out the invading Vikings, the sudden silence felt oppressive in the surroundings.

High-sided buildings of cut stone and cobbled side streets held the last echoes of their big engines for so long that he thought he was imagining it, until it finally dissipated and left him feeling almost alone. He wasn't, he knew, he had close to forty men with him, and they were all safely ensconced behind thick armour plating, and looking down the barrels of heavy machine guns and some even larger weapons to their rear. But still, despite the logical facts of being safe and protected, he still felt very much alone.

Perhaps that isolation was more about the burden of command than about the physical aspects of being lonely.

The silence he heard, or more that he felt, wasn't a true silence. There were still the ticking and clanging noises of the ten engines cooling down, as well as the echoing ambience of a town thrown into sudden silence by the absence of normal daily life; but other sounds began to creep into his consciousness.

A bird call, raucous even at a long distance away. A building alarm, an insistent bell ringing, from somewhere indeterminate due to the confusing sounds that bounced between the rows of tall stone buildings. A shout, high pitched and pleading, from somewhere up ahead. Or behind. Johnson's head whipped back and forth to try and locate the sound and not be tricked by the echo. He heard it again; a woman's voice, shouting at the top of her voice and dragging the word out excruciatingly.

It said, *help.* More precisely, it swore.

Poking his own head out of the hatch on the other spacious − or at least spacious by light tank standards − Sultan armoured car behind, Palmer's eyebrows almost met in the middle as he watched Johnson snatch off his helmet and headset and fling his head wildly from side to side.

"What the devil...?" he muttered to himself, just as the radio burst into life and he could read the lips of the man speaking.

"One Troop, form a rear guard at this position. Assault troop, advance one hundred metres and cut engines; listen for survivors," he snapped, looking in the direction of the troops he was talking to as he gave the orders. All around them, big engines barked into life and belched clouds of black smoke into the air. The four smaller tracked vehicles bucked and reared as they drove ahead, and Johnson gave a rapid order to his driver to follow, meaning to halt his small section of two vehicles at the mid-point between the Fox cars and the Spartans. Hating being a spectator again, Johnson was forced to listen to the action unfold as the light tanks blocked his view.

"Female, second floor window. Stand by," came Maxwell's clipped voice over the radio. "She's indicating something to us... contact, enemy front, wait out."

Johnson, unknown to him but watched intently by his radio operator, pressed down gently on the topmost bullet in the spare magazine on his webbing.

The rough, hardened skin of his right thumb rubbed the exposed brass smooth as he repeated the gesture over and over. He knew there was no point in demanding an update from them, even less sense in driving up to them and losing visual contact with the other half of his current fighting strength, so he had to supress the urge once more to push his way to the front of the queue and get his bayonet wet. The seconds ticked by, then the radio sparked to life again, only it wasn't what he was expecting to hear.

"Foxtrot-Three-Three-Alpha this is Foxtrot-One-Zero, contact rear," the voice rabbited, giving the information in a single word with barely a pause in between.

Momentarily torn, Johnson's logical brain kicked in to ask the question into the mic before he even knew he had decided on it.

"Foxtrot-One-Zero, stand by. Foxtrot-Five-Zero what is your situation?" He said, telling the panicking voice behind them to hold on until he knew what Maxwell was doing.

The rearguard were sealed up tight behind armour, whereas his vanguard had civilians in the open and would have to open their doors or put lives at risk.

"Twenty plus approaching, civilians preparing to come out. Enemy not responding to warnings," came Maxwell's terse reply. Behind that report were the sounds of various troopers going through the motions of their training and following the rules of engagement.

They had these rules of engagement drummed into them over and over. They could not use any more force than the minimum necessary, as ambiguous as that was, and they were told time and again to fire only aimed shots, that automatic fire could only be used against identified targets, and that a verbal warning should be given whenever possible.

Johnson knew how impractical those rules could be, even with an enemy who could hear and respond, but he also knew that his men found comfort in the repetition of training and that comfort allowed the rest of their actions to flow smoothly. Like training the cupola on a target, like calling out their firing arc and reporting ready, like asking for permission to open fire.

"Automatic fire," Maxwell announced, "go on."

The gunners, as inhumane as it would have seemed to the uninitiated, smiled as thumbs pressed down on controls and the four GPMGs sparked into boisterous life to cut down the approaching waves of shambling and screeching enemy.

The bullets these guns fired, even though they were the smallest armament their armoured column carried, unleashed their destructive power on the gathering crowd. A single GPMG, with a thousand rounds of belt-fed 7.62, could bring down a small house.

Four of them, vehicle-mounted and interlocking their arcs of fire where every other bullet streaked a fiery-red line towards their enemy, wreaked savage and unholy devastation on the slow-moving forty or so blood-streaked people stumbling at them, their mouths open and returning their own salvo of spine-numbing shrieks and hisses.

In seconds, the rippling gunfire that appeared visually like a series of lasers ceased as there were suddenly no more bodies to convert from living to dead. Johnson watched on as Maxwell organised the recovery, just as the radio sparked to life again.

"Permission to engage?" came the request in a tone of sheer panic. Panic, in Johnson's opinion, was more dangerous to his troops than enemy fire could be.

Fire could serve to rally his men against their foe.

Fire could be ineffectual, and the inaccuracy of incoming rounds could serve to raise the morale of his men.

Panic, however, did not miss. It was one hundred percent accurate, one hundred percent of the time.

They were trained for chemical warfare, as every soldier was, given the tensions with Russia. Any man or woman in uniform on the western side of the Berlin wall was on a moment's notice to pull on their thick, rubbery protection suits. They were trained to seal themselves up inside their armour to escape nuclear fallout and other such horrors of modern warfare, but the only thing that could penetrate that armour was panic.

Panic and fear, Johnson corrected himself, but fear wasn't an immediate danger.

"Negative," he responded coolly, "report."

"They're coming from bloody everywhere!" came the cry of response, "all around us," Johnson heard the irregular pounding of meaty hands on the outer hulls of the armoured car where the transmission originated, along with the mechanical whine of the car's turret rotating. Closing his eyes and holding his breath momentarily, Johnson resisted the urge to enquire as to the height of the radio operator and to opine that he was unaware shit could be stacked that tall. Instead he gave his orders very simply and calmly.

"Foxtrot-One-Zero, advance through the enemy one hundred metres and hold fast. Acknowledge?"

A pause on the other end, then, "Foxtrot-One-Zero, roger. Advance through enemy lines one hundred metres and hold," came the response of Maxwell's voice, much more calmly than whoever had spoken before. Then he heard the sound of the Jaguar engines roaring up their revs to power away. Johnson didn't want to, didn't *need* to look to know that the four heavy wheels of each vehicle would be crushing the bloody bodies of the attackers. Pushing the thought away, Johnson turned his attention back to the front. He knew that the sixteen men now moving through the town would be safe inside their vehicles, not only safe but actually offering yet more protection to the rest of the column by attracting the Screechers through the noise they would be generating,

Maxwell, in Johnson's opinion one of the very best combat leaders in the squadron, had organised one crew to dismount and source alternative transport for the civilians. Watching as the window to a van was broken, Johnson saw a trooper lift the locking pin and pull himself up behind the wheel, which he wrenched hard to snap the steering lock, then shout something at the rest of his crew, who began to push the vehicle. Johnson knew what he would be doing; handbrake off, clutch down and gearstick into second. As soon as the momentum was enough, he dropped the clutch out and the engine sparked to life.

Chapter 16

Kimberley Perkins leaned out of the second-floor window of the bank she worked in to shout at the very top of her lungs. Over and over she called for help after the stone canyons of the town centre echoed loudly with the reverberating barks of engines. From the second she heard the noise, like a squeaking, rolling thunder, despite working for the last four years in the bank where they now sought refuge, she knew that it was more than the regular noise of everyday vehicles.

Hollering until her voice gave out, she was finally rewarded when the four green wedges shot towards her on their tracks. Turning to the almost fifteen people trapped inside with her, she smiled with a confidence she didn't truly feel, but needed to display to calm them down.

She had never been able to endure people's inabilities to adapt and had always faced any situation with an almost implacable strength of character. When the screams had started, Kimberley was the only cashier working, as half the bank staff hadn't even turned up for work. She, like everyone she knew, had been following as much as she could of the emerging situation in London, but was as clueless as the others about what it meant for her.

Having been born in London and initially raised there before fate conspired to move her west along the southern coast of England, she recognised some of the streets and landmarks in the background of the news reels, and a small stab of homesickness pricked at her heart every time. When the horrific realisation of the TV blackout hit her, it was already too late.

Living in the centre of town anyway, and it being only a short walk to work, Kimberley's world was, geographically speaking anyway, incredibly small. She noticed nothing on her short walk to the bank, not even the absence of the regular amount of foot traffic, but the first hour of the day made her skin tingle with a slight feeling of dread, as the anticipated morning rush never came. After that came the sounds of sirens. In itself, the sound of a siren wasn't unexpected as the bank was in the town centre where the ambulance station, fire station and police station were all a short walk away. She didn't even hear the sirens any more, not really, since her apartment was in the same location and she had long since become accustomed to the noise.

But today was different, because the sound of sirens had been constant for ten minutes straight, and then faded to nothing. Not nothing, precisely, but a void. A vacuum. A hollow space that seemed both absent of any real information, but similarly full of noise that confused her.

That vacuum soon filled with noises which were discernible from the general cacophony, and the eyes of the none-staff of the bank began to fix on each other's as screams sounded in the town. When a half dozen people bundled in, pushing and shoving each other as they ran, and begged for help, then she finally knew it was happening.

She still didn't know what *it* was, but it was a safe bet that whatever had prevented the flow of information out of the capital had found its way to their town. It had a soundtrack, even if it didn't have a name, and the soundtrack that accompanied the disorder was riddled with screams and hisses and metallic screeches ripped from human throats.

"Upstairs, everyone, now," she called aloud as she stood, directing the staff and newcomers towards the heavy metal door that led to the secure part of the building.

"Miss Perkins," snapped the deputy assistant manager, a peevish man of her age but only half her presence. He had relished the lack of staffing that day as he took charge. "Members of the public are not allowed in the restricted part of the bank," he whined.

Before she could respond, the answer was given loud and clear from outside in a far more effective way than she could have explained.

A young man, his face a sheet of blood from a torn scrap of skin and hair that flopped over his forehead and his eyes milky white, slammed his whole body into the heavy plate glass, and slowly worked his jaw as he tried to chew his way through the impenetrable barrier that kept them safe. Everyone inside the bank froze and stared at the man, his greasy coveralls slicked red with fresh blood. But a woman joined him with the same percussive slam as her body bounced off the glass, only to return immediately and cause a long, squeaking noise to vibrate through the room, as her top lip was pulled upwards by the resistance of the glass. Her teeth were smeared red, which extended down from her mouth to discolour the light blue shirt she wore over a navy, knee-length skirt. Her eyes, the same opaque cloudy orbs as the man's, bored through to them.

"Upstairs!" Kimberley shouted again and, as though their heads were on the same piece of taught string, the two people chewing at the glass snapped their heads in perfect synchronicity to lock on to her. They needed no further encouragement, and as one, they surged for the heavy, reinforced door that was opened with a combination to swing outwards. No sooner had the first five people bundled through that door amidst shouts and noises of panic than another three loud thumps reverberate from the front window.

Kimberly was the second to last person at the door, the last man being the peevish manager for the day, who was counting people through for no particular reason she could discern.

He flinched, but did not turn to see what had caused the new noise.

He looked at Kimberley's face and slowly began to mirror her emerging look of dread. Not having the courage to turn and face whatever new horrors had arrived to shatter his orderly world, he kept his eyes down and pulled the heavy door closed.

Others in the town centre weren't so lucky. Only the banks had windows that didn't shatter and implode under the onslaught of hungry, feverishly aggressive mouths. Because the number of infected rose with each step closer towards the emergence of the virus, those attacked weren't always lucky enough to escape with an infected bite to die at home as the fever burned through their bodies. When attacked by three or four of the things, often their victims would fall where they were attacked, to be torn apart.

Looking out of the window high above the street below, Kimberley saw exactly that happen before her eyes. A woman, wearing the brightly coloured uniform of a travel agent in the style of that company's air hostesses, ran into the street screaming foully, only to be hit hard from three different directions and have the air driven from her lungs when they took her to the rough round. The three attackers bit her, clawed at her with their nails and pulled chunks of her flesh away where they could gain sufficient purchase on it.

Kimberley ignored the shouted questions, the hysterical tears and the screams of panic and confusion, which sounded from behind her, and watched as the three cannibalistic attackers stopped in perfect unison.

They just stopped, for no evident reason that she could understand, and turned their attention elsewhere as they looked for something, some*one*, else to attack. As they rose and melted away stiffly, Kimberley was left watching the bloodied and torn body of the woman, who she could see, even at that distance, had previously been adorned with a perfect face of makeup before the blood had splashed to mar the overall effect. The eyes, unclear as the two floors in height separated them, stared upwards blankly in death until the view was obscured by a sudden cloud of condensation covering the window. Kimberley, in her shock at seeing a murder in the street below her, had forgotten to breathe until that point when the part of her brain that took responsibility for such things restored order, and forced her lungs to inflate. She watched, fixed intently on the body of the woman in a state of semi-shock, as a way to cope with the screaming debates that raged behind her. She had no idea how long she remained there, minutes at least in her wide-eyed catatonia, but the next terrifying turn of events woke her to full alertness.

That same part of the brain that forced Kimberley to breathe again, not that she could know it, also kicked in to high gear in the woman lying on the street below in a large puddle of her own blood.

Thinking that she had imagined it at first, she saw the ravaged body of the woman twitch once in a full body spasm. Trying to ignore that as a trick that her confused and frightened brain was playing on her, she visibly jumped as the body convulsed electrically once more. Now convincing herself that it was a process of her dying, Kimberley rationalised what her eyes had told her brain. What she saw next could not be rationalised, nor could it be explained.

The woman, moving jerkily and uncertainly like a drunk, clambered to her feet in a very unladylike manner, which forced her tight skirt up to the tops of her thighs and flashed a swathe of skin-coloured stocking tops to the world. She didn't care, and if she had, then Kimberley would probably have found that disturbing as the priority. Should the woman be aware of anything, it would be the small loop of what Kimberley could only guess was intestine that flopped from under her white blouse to hang just below her crotch. Swallowing a mouthful of bile, she watched as the woman began to take awkward, halting steps, to follow the direction of her head turned up the street towards where the commotion had washed like a tide. What Kimberley couldn't see was the sudden milky white colour of the woman's eyeballs, and what she couldn't hear was the hissing, rasping noise she made that was quieter than the others around her, as a hole had been torn into her windpipe and it allowed some of the air to escape and lower her volume controls.

As she stumbled away from the bank and left the street below empty, Kimberley stayed glued to the window for more long minutes, until the dull roar of lots of engines echoed through the town.

Being so high up, that floor didn't have the reinforced glass of the ground and first floors, so she was able to open the window. She began to scream for help at the top of her voice and ignored the protestations of those behind her. She was finally rewarded with the four camouflaged metal wedges shooting off from their stationary points and coming towards her. Within seconds they had stopped outside the bank, and a hatch popped open for a man with a handlebar moustache under his helmet, and wide eyes. He seemed to speak to himself, then she watched as the other three tanks moved position slightly before cutting their engines. The man shouted a question up at her, forcing her to turn and call for quiet as she performed a rapid head count and turned back to the window.

"Fifteen of us," she called down, making sure to clearly enunciate each word and remove the need to repeat the information.

"Can you get out of this door?" he asked, pointing at the main entrance to the bank. She responded that they could.

"Wait there," the man said after listening to his radio, or at least she imagined that was what he did as his eyes glazed over and he placed a finger to the earphone nearest his right hand, "and cover your ears."

Then he looked forward and dropped down, pulling the hatch closed behind him.

Kimberley didn't have the luxury of time to relay that instruction, but human nature being what it was they all dropped to the ground and covered their ears, screwing their eyes shut tightly as though that would help, when the world outside and below them erupted into a storm of metal and noise and devastation. The automatic gunfire didn't last long, a few seconds at most, but the shouting that followed was more insistent than before. Getting to her feet and looking back down to street level, she saw four soldiers burst from the nearest tank and run just out of sight. The noise of an engine starting was loud in the street, but the strong voice cut through that din to give her orders.

"Move, now," it yelled, as though she were a raw recruit in need of toughening up. She turned and relayed those orders, surprising herself with how authoritarian she sounded, and saw the confidence of those orders translated into instant action as the fourteen other people ran to obey. She was the last one down the stairs, her eyes resting on the partly open drawer which she knew would contain stacks of crisp banknotes, and shook her head to will away the ridiculous and improper thought as soon as it came to her.

Running down the stairs and into the lobby of the bank, she found the others milling about uncertainly as they waited for someone to tell them what to do next.

Kimberley hurtled past all of them, pausing only to shout, "Come on!" and to spark them into life to follow. She burst through the doors and into the street, her head acquiring the noise of the engine and seeing the source for the first time. A dirty white Ford panel van, the back doors wide open and some cardboard boxes visible inside, stood thirty paces away with three soldiers waving them frantically towards them. The fifteen survivors piled in, the doors were shut, and a hand banged on the thin metal side twice.

Maxwell recalled his dismounted troopers, bar the one who had been given the responsibility of driving the van full of civilians, and Johnson watched as his assault troop made its way back toward him, comprising an additional vehicle. Nodding his appreciation for a job well done, he turned his attention back to the rear guard. Calling the Sabre troop up on the radio he asked for a report, learning that the remaining crowd of enemy had followed them slowly and were approaching their position.

"On me," he instructed, telling the drivers of the Fox cars to make the return journey through the obstructions of biting meat that used to be people. "We are leaving via an alternative route," and with that, he relayed his orders to the rest of the column and decided to get the hell out of the town.

The commandeered panel van sat neatly in between the two high-roofed tracked vehicles of Johnson's HQ troop, and the assault troop continued as vanguard. They did not stop to lay down any fire as the enemy never threatened the safety of their convoy at any point. Instead, Johnson called their retreat under a new protocol, this time meaning that they did not stop for anything and no vehicle was ever out of visual contact with those in front and behind, and at a maximum of half their vehicle's effective range of weapons fire. In a town, that meant that they were driving as fast as their tracked and heavy-wheeled mix of cars could manage, but when they hit the wider roads of the outskirts they pushed their speed up to just over fifty miles per hour.

Calling a stop at the very edge of the built-up area, Johnson faced a dilemma. That dilemma was whether to retain personal control of the tip of his spear and remain with a troop, or to return to base and debrief the civilians to formulate a longer-term plan. He knew what he should do, but that would mean leaving a fighting troop under the technical control of an officer he didn't trust to get a drinks order right. Making his decision, he dismounted his own vehicle and climbed down to approach the identical one behind it. Palmer, having heard of the SM's approach, popped the hatch and also dismounted to speak to the man away from the armour.

"SSM," he said in greeting, his face wan and serious for a change, "your suggestions?"

Johnson swallowed, keeping down the retort that flew to the tip of his tongue, and the with it the urge to slap the young man around the head. He didn't act on those feelings, however, because he recognised that the man was just emulating the behaviour of other officers. To ask the senior NCO for their suggestion was to admit to nobody that you didn't know the best way to proceed, and you were calling on the experience of a man who would know. That only offended Johnson because when Second Lieutenant Palmer used the term, it implied that he was in overall charge of the squadron. That rankled him and made his words slightly harsher than they would have been, had the boy not tried to play the boss.

"My *orders*," he began, "are that you remain here with One. Sergeant Strauss will be in charge," he added in a quieter voice as he leant forward to prevent embarrassing the man, "and your task will be to remain here until such time as our half of the column returns to base. If you are engaged during that time, then you are to ensure that no enemy survives the contact before returning. Understood?"

"Understood entirely," Palmer retorted with his aristocratic air of condescension, then he turned away, no doubt to relay *his* orders to his crew.

Strauss, the third generation of a Rhodesian migrant had, despite his name and heritage, no trace of the accent of his predecessors, but he did bear the genetic traits.

Tall and broad, uncomfortably so for a man who went to war inside a cramped metal box, his blonde hair was kept short inside his helmet.

Johnson relayed his orders, adding in the specifics that Palmer didn't need to burden himself with, lest he gain the incorrect impression that he was in charge of anything, and left feeling satisfied that those orders would be followed.

"I think these things are attracted to noise," he told Strauss, who absorbed the facts and recent events with no sign of being affected, "so I don't want to roll our armour slowly back to base and ring the diner bell. You wait for whatever crowd follows us out of town, then open up on them, 30mm too just for the noise, then get back via a longer route, and whatever you do," he added seriously, "don't let the Lieutenant do anything stupid like order another charge of the light brigade."

Strauss understood, and Johnson left with the assault troop and the borrowed van, the occupants of which had been unceremoniously told to stay quiet until they were back to base.

Strauss was a switched-on and capable man, if not a natural tactician like Johnson. He kept his four Fox armoured cars in tight formation across the carriageway with their engines running, and ordered that the hatches be closed, if only to ensure that Palmer didn't try to join in the fight, as his vehicle was the only type that couldn't bring weapons to bear from the safety of the inside.

After forty minutes the distant horizon started to show a dark smear that morphed into an oncoming line of people, all moving slowly and awkwardly. That was their target, and he intended to destroy this crowd before taking a looping journey back to base, and hopefully not to lead any more of them to the fence that ringed their camp.

The only unexpected issue was that of the two shapes out ahead of the crowd. They had pushed through at a distance the soldiers could not discern, and were now jogging ahead of them at over twice the speed of the masses. Their actions were more coordinated somehow, and they were less damaged than the others, which lent them a kind of alertness that could only spell trouble.

"Sarge?" the driver of Strauss' Fox called out to him questioningly.

"I see them, son," he said in a fatherly tone to soothe the man's nerves. "Gunner, to your front, automatic fire… go on," he said, hearing the answer given by the rapid pounding of the big 30mm cannon above their heads. Watching the road ahead, he smiled a grim smile of satisfaction as the leading monster disintegrated in a flash of red mist, leaving a single leg to cartwheel through the air before it landed wetly a good three hundred paces away from their picquet line.

"All gunners," Strauss said calmly into the radio, "automatic fire to your front. Go."

And the world on the edge of a small rural town erupted into a cacophonous, percussive hell.

Chapter 17

Peter, in a bizarre form of coping strategy that he didn't fully understand, was actually enjoying his project. Had he known more about human interactions and had a basic understanding of psychology, he might have recognised that he had gone onto a kind of dissociative state, where productivity could mask the feelings that his recent experiences had caused. Those feelings, had he had the luxury of time and safety to replay the events and the emotions that came at each step, would cripple him if he allowed them space in his brain so he simply didn't.

The events of the last week, as obvious as they were, had just happened and were now shut away in a box that he didn't have to open. It was the only way he could function.

So instead of curling up into a ball and crying like the child he was, he refused to accept that those things had happened, and gave himself a new reality to deal with. That reality was that he couldn't go home, that he was totally alone, and that he had to survive by himself. He had to stay away from people, he had to keep himself, remain as quiet as possible and wait for it all to stop spinning like crazy.

The last part even he knew was fantasy, but survival without hope wasn't survival; it was prolonging the process of dying.

He had to retain hope that someone would restore order, that the police or the army would come with guns and sticks and make everyone behave again. Even though he hadn't seen much of the world, either before or after people started biting each other, he knew that there was unlikely to be any safety anywhere else, so he elected to make a home in the place he knew best.

The first day was spent attempting to weather-proof his new accommodation, having shivered throughout the entire night previously due to the wind whistling through the cracks on the boards. His way of rectifying this was to rig a series of heavy canvas sheets and nail them into place using the tools he had taken from the shed. These sheets, which he thought had once been ground sheets for large tents, were pulled tightly into position, then nailed into the wood at the corners at regular intervals, so that they formed a secure section that the wind couldn't penetrate. Inside that section Peter laid down an even bed of hay, then another of the heavy sheets which he had folded over three times lengthways, and he rolled himself on that makeshift bed until he had ironed out the worst of the lumps with his back. Climbing back down the short ladder, he rigged up a simple rope pulley system to allow him to place things inside the large plastic bucket on one end of the rope, before climbing up to his hideout in safety to pull on the rope to raise his haul without the risk of falling off the ladder.

Finishing these two tasks before his growling stomach reminded him of the other basic needs, he stopped to dangle his legs off the edge of his bedroom and he ate crisps and chocolate once again. Another thing he didn't know was the likely side-effects of eating sugar-rich, processed foods when his body wasn't used to them, mixed with the absence of any useful carbohydrates and fibre. The resulting feelings as soon as he had finished his snack, made him realise another need he had failed to cater for.

Peter had, at times, been taken hunting and fishing with his father. Those trips, often accompanied by cans of cheap high-strength lager, often imparted some knowledge to the boy. His father didn't overtly intend this, more that he just spouted more and more rubbish and platitudes the more alcohol he imbibed. But some things had stayed with Peter and they came back to him piece by piece.

Shape, smell and sound were the main aspects which interested him now; the very fundamentals of camouflage. If a predator made noise or showed its recognisable body to prey, the prey would run away before the hunter could strike. If that hunter approached from downwind, then the prey would also run as soon as it detected the danger.

"You can tell a lot from an animal by its shit," his father had told him once, bending to examine a patch of small, brown pellets. "What's that?"

"Rabbit?" Peter guessed.

"Yes," his father responded, casting his eyes up and scanning the hedgerow closest to them before raising a finger and pointing at a patch of smoothed grass that was shorter than the rest of the field, "and that is why rabbits are just food for other things," he intoned. "You don't shit where you eat."

With that, he raised his shotgun and took a snapshot at a tight cluster of three rabbits bursting from cover to dash for the safety of their underground warren, and he rolled two of them over in broken ruin with a single shot.

As the pain in his belly worsened, Peter's mind ran over and over these concepts of predator and prey until a shocking realisation hit him. All the pearls of wisdom and un-fatherly advice he had been given had to be ignored.

Ignored because the advice was given to him as though he were the predator, and not the prey.

He had to stay downwind of *them,* and keep his senses alert for *their* smell.

He had to keep *his* ears tuned to the hissing, screeching noises they made to accompany the irregular shambling of their movements.

He had to be observant of others, and learn to tell in an instant whether they were friend or foe.

He had to learn to be a clever bit of prey, or he would become a meal for a predator.

Unable to contain the roiling in his intestines any longer, Peter ran to the small river that flowed along the outer-edge of the farm and dropped his trousers to void himself messily into the shallow water. He watched in mixed awe and disgust as the cloudy patch of water flowed downstream to dissolve and dissipate in the gentle flow. Satisfied that his father had finally taught him something useful, he cleaned himself in the river and returned to his lodgings.

Now that the issue of shelter had been appropriately addressed, Peter turned his attention towards water. The barn he was in had a water collection barrel at the foot of the drainpipe just outside the doors, but he didn't trust that. Walking a short distance to the nearest outside tap on the wall of a building, he turned it to be instantly rewarded with a jet of clean water. It didn't occur to him that this magical, endless supply might one day cease to function. After shelter and water came defence; something which Peter had already considered, given his instinctive thought to bring not only the bent pitchfork that he now had an unbreakable affinity with, but also his father's shotgun. That gun, with its long twin barrels, was taller than Peter when he stood alongside it, and although he knew the fundamentals of how it worked from watching it fired and reloaded so many times, he couldn't manhandle the long gun with enough strength to bring it to bear. Glancing between the shotgun and the pitchfork, Peter decided to make some necessary modifications to his small arsenal, and to make them slightly more user-friendly for his size.

One of his favourite places on the farm was the workshop. Like their own shed back at the house, it was stocked with tools, and benches with vices and machines that he didn't understand. He loved that dirty, oily smell of the building that brought hints of the outside in, given that any tractors in need of repair were driven into the empty section of the shop and worked on under the bank of strip-lighting high overhead.

Peter flicked on the light switch just inside the door, hearing the metallic twanging noise it made as the electricity burst into life. Carrying only the pitchfork, he walked towards the woodwork vice on the nearest bench and spun the handle to open it wider. Then he nestled the long wooden handle of the tool in the neck of the vice between the two scarred blocks of hard wood. Cinching the handle tight, he went to the wall where the wooden backboards had been painted white to allow for the tool outlines to be marked clearly in black pen. He didn't know if that was to make it easier to find everything, or just to keep track of what they had and dissuade workers from stealing. Selecting a thin-bladed hacksaw, Peter nestled the blade against the metal holding the bent outer tine of the tool, as he stood looking down the length of it. Then he carefully drew back the blade in a straight line a few times to create a furrow that the saw could sit in. With that done, he began to use the hacksaw in long draws, both forwards and backwards, in a rhythmic pattern.

Let the blade do the work, a voice from his memory told him, *don't force it.*

He didn't force it, and the blade had soon eaten its way through to the other side of the thin prong and he watched it fall gently to the floor with a tinkling sound. Assessing his handiwork, Peter though that the now three-pronged pitchfork looked odd and lop-sided, so he loosened the vice and spun it over to repeat the process with the odd tine. When the second tinkling noise of metal hitting concrete sounded, he was far more satisfied with the results and was looking at a more streamlined version of the tool. Restoring the hacksaw carefully to its allocated slot on the wall, Peter selected a metal file and rounded off the rough sawn edges of metal. He worked like an artist creating something, moving the file in meticulous, measured strokes to create a smooth edge that wouldn't cut or catch.

Reapplying that level of attention to the other side, he turned his attention to the tips of the curved prongs and worked at them to elongate and sharpen the points.

His tongue popped out of one side of his mouth as he worked, lost in the attention to detail that the task allowed him to apply. Standing tall and happy with the two business ends of the now adapted weapon, he restored the file to its proper place and selected a short, rectangular wood saw, which he used to remove the bottom foot of spare handle.

Taking both the pitchfork and the off-cut of wood to one of his most favourite things, he clamped the weapon into the grips of the big lathe and pressed the green button to start it spinning.

The wall beside the lathe had two distinct sides, each with their tools marked out in the same fashion as everywhere else. Selecting a scooped chisel from the woodworking side, Peter rounded the end of the handle in a few seconds, then stopped the machine with the dirty red button and waited for it to cycle down. Swapping it for the off-cut, he worked more delicately by first rounding the cut end, then reducing the overall thickness of the piece so that it better fit his small grip. Taking it out and replacing the chisel, he dropped the cut handle into the vice once more and used a hand-turned drill to bore a hole directly downwards, deep into the wood from the most tapered end. Picking up the discarded metal prong of the fork that hadn't been bent, he used the hacksaw once again to render it into a single curved piece, then used a ball hammer to straighten out the curve. To finish his piece, he forced the single spike down into the hole drilled into the handle, using the hammer to tamp it down hard into place and blunting the end. He rectified this by retrieving the file before using the hammer again to straighten the two remaining prongs of his fork.

Each time he had selected a different tool, he had painstakingly replaced the one he was using before picking up another. This was not a side-effect of Peter's upbringing, where he had lived in permanent fear of punishment, but an indication of his ordered, logical mind instead.

When he had finished and cleared up the workshop, he switched off the lights and went back outside, carrying his two weapons. His trusty stickers, as he called them on a whim; so named for their primary purpose of sticking bad people through the eyes.

Chapter 18

"Next," called Sergeant Croft as he waited for the well-dressed young woman to shuffle along in the line to approach his desk. "Name?" he enquired tiredly, having been inundated with another fifteen civilians, or more like refugees, on the return of half of the troops to complement the already steady trickle of inbound human traffic.

"Kimberley Perkins," Kimberley said, feeling annoyed at having to wait in line to get any answers, after the uncomfortable hour they had been bounced around inside the back of the van. It wasn't that she was ungrateful for their sudden and unexpected rescue, but she was rather in need of some information that could help her rationalise everything that had happened that morning to lead her there, wearing just her working clothes and having to abandon everything she owned, as the thought of going back to the town was the least sensible thing she could imagine.

"Miss, Mrs or Ms?" Croft enquired without looking up from his clipboard.

"It's Miss," she replied, reading the list upside down and answering the next three questions with, "twenty five years old, bank clerk, and I'm here alone," she said, prompting an annoyed look of pursed lips to cross Croft's face as he finally glanced up to let her know he was annoyed.

That look of annoyance quickly melted away in embarrassment as he found himself looking up into a well-defined face framed by dishevelled brunette hair in tight curls.

"Thank you, Miss Perkins," he said as he averted his gaze again, "if you wouldn't mind waiting to this side of the hall now, and we can process everyone through to give you some answers very shortly."

She was used to that. People looked at her, then looked away out of shame or embarrassment, but mostly to stop themselves from staring. She was not ugly, nor was she overly disfigured, but the scar that marked the left side of her face was puckered and slightly more pink than the rest of her face. The scar, a cruel reminder of a past best forgotten, served as a way to unintentionally repel people. Although she had grown accustomed to the few predictable responses people usually gave her on seeing the scars for the first time, each occurrence did nothing to remove the stab of pain and shame she felt at recognising it. She'd experimented with her hairstyle in an effort to hide it, but had decided that the Farrah Fawcett look was just too much work. Absent-mindedly tipping her head to bring her hair down over her left shoulder to obscure where the rippled skin went over her ear, she thanked the soldier in a formal tone and followed the directions she was given.

When they had first arrived at the army base, which she had discovered as such by blinking into the sunlight after the gloom of the rear of the van, to find herself staring directly at a large white sign denoting that the fenced enclosure was, indeed, an army camp, she had watched as the other people she had shared her escape with had hugged and thanked the soldiers, who all seemed to want to line up for the attention. Some made a direct line for her, seeing a tall and slim young woman, but almost all of them shied away when they saw the mess on one side of her face.

Same story as anywhere else, she thought, *it's like I'm contagious.*

She had asked to speak to whomever was in charge and was politely yet firmly instructed to wait with the others in a small holding room by the gate. The room was too small for all of them, much as the rear of the van had been, but she endured it for as long as she was able, until they were brought forwards one by one to give them their details.

Having waited in three separate lines for the purpose of simply waiting with a feeling of achievement, they were herded through to another building where there were big metal tins of hot water.

"Tea," yelled the sergeant pointing at the first one and giving it a rap with his knuckle as he passed, "and coffee," he called, dinging the other one and making a noise that sounded less echoing than the first.

Kimberley, seeing the masses head towards the tea urn, opted for the coffee as the line was shorter and the chance of running out before it was her turn was greatly reduced by the simple evidence she had interpreted through logic and hearing.

"Take a seat, everyone," the soldier said in a raised voice to cut through the din of conversation regarding sugar and milk, "and I'll try to tell you what's been going on."

That got everyone's attention, and the rush to take their hastily made drinks to a spare seat became the number one priority for people.

"As you have found out today, the UK has gone more than a little off the deep end," he began, apparently attempting to make light of the events. "Three days ago, our command structure in London went down. By that I mean that it stopped broadcasting radio signals and picking up the phone. We are, all of us, in the dark about what is currently going on." Realising that he wasn't filling people with confidence, the soldier cleared his throat and tried to pick up the tempo in his voice, which was in danger of becoming dreary.

"The disease is believed to have originated somewhere near central London a week ago and has spread rapidly outward from the capital to outlying areas. As of yesterday, it has hit our county."

Tell us something we don't already know, Kimberley thought unkindly to herself.

"Reports from other areas of the country indicate that there are outbreaks further north and west, also…" he paused, prompting total silence in the room, interrupted only by the gurgling of the overused tea urn, "…also we have received radio contact from the continent and our bases in Germany. They appear to be engaged in heavy fighting with the same enemy over there," he said with reluctant finality.

"So, what do we do?" asked a woman hesitantly from the front row of chairs.

"You wait here, and we will keep you protected and informed of the situation as and when updates arise," answered the man woodenly, using the words in such a fashion that made Kimberley think of the terminology she had heard once.

Bullshit baffles brains, she told herself, *bullshit baffles brains.*

~

As Kimberley and all the other civilians were herded out of the mess hall where they had been assembled, a burbling, rolling thunder headed towards them from the gate. The group watched the return of the four-wheeled tanks and the one squeaking metal wedge that stood alone, as it was only one of the small convoy moving on tracks.

They rolled straight past the small crowd who, in the predictable behaviour of humans all over the world, stopped to stare at the display of mechanical and military might that is a line of light reconnaissance tanks.

Their staring wasn't just in the usual vein of normal people watching the rare sight of military vehicles, because their faces were registering horror and disgust.

Sergeant Strauss, his head and shoulders protruding from the open hatch of the lead vehicle, offered the crowd a smile of greeting that spoke of duty more than any genuine emotion of happiness. Seeing their looks of repulsion and horror, his own smile faded as he wondered what he could have done to cause such a response. They passed quickly just as one thin man turned and fountained vomit over the shoulders of two other people, who shrieked in response.

Strauss turned his eyes back to the front and waited until the small convoy came to a noisy stop outside the building being used as the squadron's temporary command centre. Only then did he see the source of the looks his small column had received.

"Jesus bloody Christ," he groaned out loud as he looked at the side of his own four-wheeled car in the lead. Looking down the line he saw that the others were just as bad if not worse, but the lower-bodied, tracked vehicle of the Sultan command car looked as though it had driven through a butcher's shop, then a clothing store, then back through a slaughterhouse.

Thick gore and patches of material from the clothing the things had been wearing were splattered all over the wheels and axles, and now dripped or fell off in small chunks whilst the cars were stationary.

"Fuck me," he muttered to himself in disgust and disbelief, "Corporal McGill?"

"Sarge?" McGill answered from inside his mount.

"Get all of these cleaned down," he instructed, "thoroughly. I don't want to find any fingers or anything in my running gear."

"Sarge," McGill answered simply, in a tone that conveyed his understanding and intention to comply as instructed.

Strauss watched as the cars revved up and moved away to leave him in a thick cloud of rich exhaust fumes. Turning back after the cars had rolled away, he found himself beside Lieutenant Palmer, who was wearing a face of thinly veiled annoyance.

Strauss knew that their brief interaction of earlier that day would bring with it a reckoning at some point, which he knew would not be now, as Johnson would be less than impressed with a pissing contest when there was work to be done. But he strongly suspected that Palmer had other ideas.

Setting off for the door at the same time, the smaller stature of the junior officer forced him to step faster than Strauss' long gait to make the door before he did. T he sergeant smiled to himself, anticipating the cutting report the Lieutenant would give about him, and mentally prepared his bingo card.

He was certain that the word 'insolent' would make an appearance, as the man had used it at least twice already, along with 'disobey orders', 'mere Sergeant' and his personal wildcard of 'protest'.

He did not have to wait long, nor was he disappointed with his predictions as the anticipated words almost tumbled from him.

"Sergeant Major," he snapped peevishly as he strode in, making Johnson, who was hatless yet still wearing his webbing, look up from a table covered in maps and squint his eyes through the cigarette smoke at the intrusion.

"What can I do for you, Lieutenant?" Johnson asked slowly, as though he knew that whatever was troubling the young officer so much wouldn't feature high on his own list of priorities.

"Sergeant Major," he said once more as he glanced around the room at the busy soldiers in earshot, "perhaps we should retire to have this conversation in private?"

"Lieutenant Palmer," Johnson said tiredly as he cast his eyes back down to the map, "I'm waiting for your report and have plenty of other things to be doing, so if you please, Sir?"

Johnson's tone and good manners should have told the young man where to pitch his response, but instead, the years of entitled upbringing and reinforced classicism exerted itself without a single care for the environment and situation.

"Very well," Palmer began, "I must protest, Sergeant Major, about the behaviour of Sergeant Strauss," he began, totally misreading the dangerous look on the SSM's face. "He deliberately disobeyed my orders to retreat and insisted on remaining in the open after I had given the command to withdraw, and *then*," his voice rose half an octave, "when I gave orders to return to base, he ignored me entirely and led the troop on a wild jaunt all over the county," Johnson shuddered internally at the way he pronounced the word as *Kine-ty*, "and, furthermore, had the audacity to presume to give me orders!"

Johnson sighed and stood up straight. He was a man who observed the proper way of things, even in wartime or when the world turned itself upside down like a snowglobe filled with body parts, so his next words were, for him, a marked indicator of the stress of the situation.

"Lieutenant, perhaps you're right," he said, seeing the man almost retract his chin in confusion, "we should have this conversation in private." With that, he nodded to a Corporal who muttered words of instruction for the others to leave the room.

"Sergeant Strauss?" the SSM added, "please wait outside."

Strauss, his expression unreadable, stamped to attention and took his leave of the room.

Palmer hadn't recognised the simple display of power Johnson had just treated him to, and he lacked the experience of working with other men to know that his implied request for the room to be cleared was obeyed not out of fear of punishment by the more senior soldier, but out of respect for the man and his rank. Further demonstration of Johnson's respect for the authority of rank was that he gave his response to Palmer in relative privacy.

Relative being the operative word, because not even a hardened shelter could have stopped his raised voice from letting everyone within a twenty-yard radius know his thoughts on the matter.

"Lieutenant," he began, "what were my last words to you before I left you in *nominal* charge of the detachment?"

Palmer's chin flapped open and closed, unable to decide which retort to use first. The time it took him to think of a response gave Johnson the incorrect sense that he believed the first question to have been taken as rhetorical.

"To remind you, Sir," he continued mockingly, "I left Sergeant Strauss in command of the detachment with my orders to follow to the letter, as I would expect him to do. But you, Sir, had to try and take over, am I right?"

"Sergeant Major, I really must prote…"

"No, Sir," barked the bigger man, "you must not protest. You must not give orders. You must not override my instructions to the men and you must *not* ever be under the impression that you know enough about anything to take charge."

Johnson's voice had grown louder and louder with each sentence, until his final word on the subject left a ringing, reverberating boom that assaulted Palmer's senses and made him flinch.

Outside, the words only slightly muffled, Strauss ticked off his bingo card with the anticipated words.

"But," Palmer managed weakly, "in front of the men, for a mere Sergeant to…"

"*Mere Sergeants*, Lieutenant, are all that stand between the enemy and junior officers. They are also often all that stands between the men and junior officers. Try to remember that, Sir," Johnson said in a lower voice that was more fatherly.

"From now on, just to be absolutely clear, your only job is to watch and learn. If you can't do that, Sir, I will have to ask you to take up duties managing the civilians."

That last statement seemed to shock some sense into the man.

"That won't be necessary, Sergeant Major," he said in a small voice, "but if I may offer a suggestion?"

Johnson fixed him with a stern look but nodded.

"If, perhaps, I was privy to those instructions, then I would know not to try and change them. Simply a suggestion, Sergeant Major," he said with unconvincing deference, then turned and left the room to walk ignominiously through the assembled men with his eyes cast down.

Johnson, left alone for a few brief seconds of self-reflection, had to admit that the privileged little prick had something of a point. Also, said prick might actually learn how to manage men and wage warfare against the Queen's enemies if he understood the orders he gave and, more importantly, why he gave them.

Hearing his name shouted in summons, Strauss went back inside.

"Tell me," Johnson instructed.

"We gunned down the first wave, moved forward and repeated, then withdrew and held until a third wave came. Mix of thirty-mil and GPMP. After that," he shifted and cleared his throat, "the Lieutenant decided that it was time to go home."

"He lost his bottle?" Johnson asked quietly.

"Can't say, Sarn't Major," Strauss said woodenly, "but we had a difference of opinion when I ordered the troop to engage the last wave coming from the town."

"And then another when you took the long way back?" Johnson asked with a raised eyebrow.

"Very much so," he said, "did the, er... did the Lieutenant say anything else about me?" he asked timidly, making Johnson glare at the man to try and determine the true meaning of the question.

"Other than the fact that you disobeyed his orders, Sergeant? No. He did not, but perhaps a lesson in how to manage officers is in order for you?"

"Very good, Sarn't Major," he said, with a ghost of a smile on his face.

"Anything else?" Johnson asked.

"Actually, yes," Strauss said as he relaxed and scratched his chin, "the Screechers aren't all the same."

That got Johnson's full attention. "Explain," he said tersely.

"They seemed to be following a leader, every time they came," Strauss said, "when they got close, one or two would break out ahead of the crowd and run instead of walk, like they were faster or smarter... stupid really because they were easy to pick off, but I'd be a lot more worried if they came at us in the open without our armour..."

He trailed off, leaving the implication unsaid. Johnson put that fact to one side for now, not that he was overly eager to be amongst the Screechers unless he was behind armour.

"And no sign of being followed back here?" the SSM asked with obvious stress behind the words.

"Nothing," he said with a hint of pride, "two ambushes put in on the way back, done in silence, no sign."

"Good work," Johnson responded before looking at his watch, "your troop has night duty, so get some rest."

He watched as the man marched out, then the others filed back in to resume the tasks they'd been performing before they had been sent away so as not to hear. Johnson was left thinking again, only this time about tactics. Being an armoured squadron, they weren't in the habit of training for being followed and how to ambush their own trail as the infantry did; they were more accustomed to using their advance reconnaissance vehicles, the faster and more agile Spartans of the assault troop, to lure enemy armour into a position their Foxes had smothered with their heavy 30mm cannons. Strauss' comment that he had stopped to ambush their own trail was logical and sensible, ensuring that he didn't unwittingly lead a whole crowd of the things to their door. That thought prompted him to issue a standing order to the room for dissemination.

"Spread the word," he told them, "I need silence as far as we can manage on base. Noise and light discipline during darkness; no point in advertising our presence to them, is there?"

And as soon as he said it, he knew their long-term survivability depended on their ability to find somewhere else to be.

Chapter 19

Peter had no high metal chain-link fences to hide behind. He had no armoured vehicles to keep him safe from biting teeth and clawing nails. He had no light artillery or heavy machine guns. He had no comrades.

He was totally alone, living in a breezy hay loft with a dwindling supply of food and was armed with a modified pitchfork and a shotgun that was too large for him to use.

On the third morning of his new life he woke with the morning sun and went about his new morning routine. He brushed his teeth and put on clean underwear, then did his early chores before eating. He went to the river and checked the three static lines to see if they had yielded anything overnight. One had, but the catch was small. It had also perished on the line, no doubt exhausting itself to go belly up after fighting against the hook caught in its mouth, but Peter would not say no to fresh fish. Refreshing the lines with a new worm on each hook, selected from the plentiful supply he found from lifting any of the small hen houses nearby, he reset his water traps and carried his pathetically small haul back to the barn.

He was young, but he wasn't stupid. He never struck a flame inside the hay barn as he knew that fire and dry hay tended not to mix.

Actually, he corrected himself, *they mixed a little too well. They got on like a house on fire.*

Using the electric four-ring cooker inside the small office-cum-kitchen to warm a frying pan, he messily cracked in two eggs as he ran a sharp knife along the underside of the small fish to remove its guts. Chopping off the head and the tail and splaying it open, he scraped out the spine and the little bones running off it and threw the fish in with the eggs. Putting all the waste to one side for the chickens, because those horrible things ate whatever he gave them, he allowed the pan to cool before he ate the contents straight from the cooking surface with a spoon.

Finished, he took his pan outside and turned on the tap which gushed a heavy, almost pressurised stream of water onto the dry, pale concrete. Peter didn't know that the flow was so strong because those few outside taps ran straight from the mains water, nor did he care, but he had learned that if he turned the tap on full, the flow was hard enough to dislodge anything that he had burnt onto the pan and blast it clean, ready for the next usage.

His stomach full, biology began to let him know that the effects on his digestive system were imminent. Going to the place he had chosen for his toilet, he did the things he needed to do. For some reason unknown to him he chose not to use the actual working toilet on the farm, and instead, the spot he had chosen had some logic to it, as it was the furthest place downstream he went to fish, and hence in his mind did not contaminate the river that provided him with a source of food.

Something in his mind had switched and told him that he had to turn his back on the safety of home and its modern trappings, even if he didn't realise he was still fully embracing those same modern trappings, just on the slightly juxtaposed setting of the farm.

If he had been more aware, maybe more educated or just more experienced in general life, then he would have recognised that it wasn't modern comforts he was escaping or avoiding, but just the house he had lived in. He had lost his sister and father to some unknown fate, and his mother had become a killer and forced him to do something that he felt guilty about.

He didn't feel guilty about killing her, but he did feel terrible guilt that he didn't feel guilty about it. That absence of guilt, the lack of any feeling about killing his own mother, burned at him deep inside, but his only way to deal with that was to bury it.

To deny it ever happened.

To close the door on the event, on the truth, and never go back to it.

That was how his young, fragile mind coped with what had happened to him.

Still early, he returned to the barn and put everything in order by making his bed and policing up his rubbish and empty wrappers to get rid of them. Something in his head, perhaps the lesson on smell betraying prey to predator, had told him that he needed to eradicate the smell of food from where he lived so as not to attract anything to him.

That same logic was what led to his morning toilet routines, and what made him naturally difficult to hunt.

Going for his morning lap of the farm to make sure everything was as he expected, he ignored the now pained and somehow annoyed lowing of the tall-backed black and white cattle who lumbered slowly towards the metal gateway when he walked by. He didn't stop, and he walked quicker to get himself out of their eye line so that they quieted down. He turned a corner behind a brick building where the pigs were kept, what few of them there were, and he saw that they had already gone out of their shelter to enjoy the early morning in the field. Their small trotters had turned an expanding cone of the grass away from the building into a swathe of dry dirt in honour of the deep mud they had created in the wetter weather.

Peter walked into the small lean-to, basically a three-sided shed with a roof, and bent down to pick up a bag of feed. Straining and pushing his legs to haul the long, cylindrical bag up, he walked awkwardly towards the fenced field whilst leaning his head to the left to see where he was going. Tipping a quarter of the bag as he sidestepped to the left in an ungainly way, he poured the brown pellets into the long trough, to be rewarded with the thundering noise of small feet running, overlaid with the insistent grunting of a dozen pigs as they pushed their snouts into the food.

Retreating to restore the bag to the lean-to, he cast an eye over the other bags and guessed at the nearly four and a half months of food he had left for them.

One bag, he thought to himself, *four days… thirty-three bags…*

He thought hard, first dividing the total number in half and then half again, then using his fingers to come up with the rough estimate. Quite why he planned to keep feeding the pigs and other animals when nobody else had stayed behind to look after them, he didn't know, but he knew he needed to have a purpose. Peter's purpose, he decided, was to keep the farm running when his father and the others had all gone.

There was nothing he could do for the cows, not to milk them anyway because the big dairy machinery took three grown men to operate twice a day, and not to feed them because the grass was plentiful and would be for months to come. The pigs had feed and were doing just fine with access to the building and their shiny tin arcs in the field. The chickens were much easier as their feed was far more plentiful, because they ate the corn that was in the tall, aluminium silos. That supply of corn was seemingly endless, which meant that the chickens would last longer than the cows or the pigs, and that saddened Peter because he hated the chickens.

Finishing his rounds with the animals, he went back to the barn. Propping his sticker, the once-pitchfork he was secretly very proud of, against the wide doorway he climbed the ladder to sit in his den, where he pulled out a book and worked on his reading.

After a lazy afternoon fishing before his second round of the farm later that day, he retired to the barn for another makeshift meal before tucking himself down in his shelter for the night.

That evening, just as the sun set fully, the rolling noise of the pained cattle, who were calling pitifully in the field, made him release his grip on the soft lamb pressed to his cheek, and wrap the pillow around his ears to block out the sounds of discomfort that he was powerless to stop.

~

"Sir!" came the panicked call that ripped SSM Johnson from his sleep. He had finally turned in around zero-one-twenty, after hours spent planning possible priority and non-priority missions as well as war-gaming through various situations, and theorising on the enemy's capabilities. Betraying years of soldiering, he rubbed his eyes once and blinked away the sleep to look at his watch, realising that the thing he had called sleep was, in fact, a little under three hours.

"What is it, Trooper?" he croaked, then cleared his throat and followed up his words with, "Report."

"Sir, the fence, Sir…" gasped the young soldier in panic, "they're fucking everywhere!"

Johnson looked at the trooper, Nevin. His eyes were as wide as saucers and he couldn't keep his feet still.

Johnson took a deep breath and held it, then blew it out to signify that the waking-up process was complete. He swung his legs sideways off the cot where he had elected to get some sleep, and poked his feet into his boots, which he laced quickly before he stood to fasten his trousers and shrug himself into his smock and webbing, before picking up his helmet and weapon. Nodding to the agitated Trooper Nevin, he followed the younger man's lead to go out into the cool night air. Covering the distance to the gate at double-time, he soon found himself face to face with Sergeant Strauss, who had rested his Sabre troop and gone back on stag in the time before Johnson had even got something to eat, let alone had any sleep.

"Sir?" Strauss said in confusion as he recognised the big man jogging out of the darkness towards him.

"Sergeant," he responded, "what's the situation?"

"We've, er," he said as he glanced between Johnson and Nevin, "we've got a crowd of them come to the fence. There was one of the faster ones here first and a trooper shot it," he said, glancing again at Nevin, who seemed to know that he had jumped the gun by deciding to fetch help without having been instructed to do so.

"Sergeant," Johnson asked calmly, "did my orders about noise discipline not filter down to the men?"

"They did," Strauss answered equably, "but the shot was necessary. The bloody thing was scaling the fence like a spider monkey."

That silenced any further protest from the senior NCO, who glanced towards the fence-line which was out of sight to him at that distance in the dark.

"And the others?" Johnson asked as he turned back to him, "Are they slower like before?"

"Yes," Strauss told him, "follow the leader again," his words making Johnson nod pensively.

"Fix bayonets, dispatch the *followers* quietly," Johnson told him.

"Orders already given," Strauss said, looking acidly past the SSM at Nevin. "Trooper, did I give you permission to leave your post?"

"No, Sarge," Nevin replied. "but I thought you'd need the Sarn't Major for…"

"If I needed the Sarn't Major, you useless bag of wind, I'd send for the Sarn't Major, would I not?"

Nevin danced on the spot again, as though he was desperate for the toilet or was standing on ground that only he found uncomfortably hot.

"Fuck me sideways with a deck chair, Nevin," Johnson snarled, "did your mother have any children who survived?"

Nevin, even in the low light, gave him a visibly shocked look.

"I shall spell it out for you, Trooper," he said in a savagely mocking tone. "Fix your fucking bayonet, reach down with your right hand and check you still have a pair of balls."

He paused to apply a gentle slap to the specific area and was rewarded with an instant sound of a man slightly winded. "Report to your fucking post and start sticking Screechers in the fucking eyes. GO!"

Noise discipline be damned, Johnson wanted to tear his own strip off the waste of oxygen that passed for one of Strauss' troopers before the sergeant got his own turn. As the terrified trooper stumbled off into the dark towards the enemy, simultaneously proving that orders had to be obeyed and that the dead were less frightening to even the weakest soldier in their squadron than the SSM was in a foul mood, Johnson realised that he could hear the low moaning sounds interspersed with hisses and the occasional screeching noise.

Those screeches, usually ripped from the tortured throat of one of the things when it came face to face with a living person, were mostly being cut short, which he hoped was due to the application of eight inches of steel bayonet.

"Night vision?" he asked Strauss.

"Maxwell's got it sorted by your Sultan. Thermal camera is good for nothing because these things don't give off heat. The image intensifiers are helping," Strauss told him, meaning that the relief troop sergeant, which was assault troop under the leadership of sergeant Maxwell, was using a portable set of light-enhancing goggles at the line where the vehicles were arrayed.

Johnson thanked Strauss and left him to do his work as he turned and double-timed towards the hulks of the armoured vehicles, which he knew would be ready to open up with their four GPMGs, should their quiet tactics not prove sufficient to stem the flow of attackers.

"Maxwell," Johnson hissed as he approached.

"Here, Boss, on your right," Maxwell answered, directing the SSM towards him. He had the heavy set of goggles pressed to his face, telling Johnson that he had directed him towards his position by sound alone as he concentrated.

"What have we got, Simon?" he asked, using the sergeant's first name in a rare display of camaraderie which he didn't often let people see.

"About a hundred of them, tops," Maxwell reported, "first one came in, screeching like a bitch on heat, and the fucking thing jumped halfway up the fence and began to climb, so Swinton slotted the bastard. After that, his bloody pals showed up in force. The boys are slotting them through the fence easily for now, but if another one of those faster fuckers comes at us where we aren't defending, then we won't know if it's inside."

Maxwell didn't say anything that Johnson hadn't instantly intuited from the quick verbal report, but the truth of his words was still stabbing its harsh reality into his brain like the shower scene in Psycho.

"Too much perimeter," Johnson answered almost poetically, "not enough soldiers."

"That's the long and the short of it," Maxwell answered.

Shaking away the longer-term problems, Johnson asked for the goggles. Maxwell handed them over and the SSM's world turned a bright green colour that carried with it a high-pitched whine. He saw troopers methodically placing the tips of their fixed bayonets to the faces chewing at the fence and thrusting forwards, then stepping smartly aside to repeat the process. Looking further afield, he saw no second wave or reinforcements coming to support the vanguard of the infected dead.

"When that's cleared," Johnson said, "your troop take point and One Troop will stand down. I'll have Two Troop roused."

Maxwell accepted and acknowledged his orders simply, mentally preparing to push his men up and dismount to monitor the fence line with their personal weapons. It always hurt an armoured cavalryman to leave his mount, but needs must, he told himself. Johnson jogged away from the front line, stepping smartly into the soldiers' barrack block, and quietly ordered another troop of soldiers usually equipped with four Fox armoured cars to deploy as infantry with their Sterling sub-machine guns, loaded and safetied, and their bayonets fixed.

The darkness was a time for the wet work, and Johnson had no clue how many nights they could keep it up for.

First order of business tomorrow, he told himself firmly, *reconnaissance of a defensible position.*

Chapter 20

By morning, and having enjoyed no more sleep, Johnson was slightly irritable. His irritability was not helped by the fact that close to one hundred bodies were piled up against the perimeter fence and the civilians were not accustomed to such sights.

None of them was accustomed to anything like it, he admitted to himself, but soldiers of the British Army were expected to be made of far sterner stuff than your average Joe.

Deciding that he could only deal with one of those pressing issues at once, he decided to allow the young Lieutenant the opportunity to be useful.

Useful, that was, in a setting other than combat, where his lack of experience and poor judgement could lead to the lives of the men being endangered. Striding to the mess hall, where the men having just been relieved from their night duties were tiredly eating a subdued breakfast, he returned the nods from the few men and NCOs who offered them, pretending not to notice the others who avoided his gaze, so that they were spared from having to acknowledge him. Making his way directly to the only man sitting alone, his back to the room in a display of mixed fear and arrogance, he cleared his throat and spoke in low tones.

"Good morning, Lieutenant," Johnson said, "when you're done, if you could oblige me with something?"

Palmer rose, drained the dregs of his china cup, and turned to face the SSM.

"Good morning," he drawled through a half smile, seeming to infer that their heated exchange from the previous day hadn't happened, "ready now, Sergeant Major, how can I be of service?"

Grateful that the officer was complying, although annoyed that he automatically left the cup and plate on the table for someone else to pick up after him, he explained as he walked towards the exit doors.

"If you could, Sir," he said, "I need you to keep the civilians inside whilst the men finish the clean-up operation," he said as they stepped outside, and he gestured at the far gate where dark mounds had piled up in places. As he squinted towards the fence, he saw that at least three figures were stumbling across the open grassland towards their base and would soon be on them and in need of dispatching. Just then, Johnson knew that they had to move, and quickly. Remembering that he was still with the young officer, he turned to face him again.

"Sir?"

"Right away, SSM," he said, choosing not to take his tasking to the civilians as a banishment. "What is the official line?"

"The official line, Sir?" he said in confusion, "we tell them the truth."

Palmer thought for a second, then nodded sagely and turned to make his way towards the building that had been used to house their refugees.

Johnson watched him walk away for a dozen paces, then turned on his own heel to stride towards the gate at a fast march.

"Povey, 'ware right," he snapped at a trooper who was closest to a Screecher approaching the fence. Trooper Povey looked to the SSM, then to his right, then hopped backwards to settle himself ready for the thrust of the bayonet that dispatched the dead woman who had shuffled up to his position as his back was turned. Johnson paused for a beat, seeing that his men had reacted instantly to their new situation, regardless of their 'day' jobs on civvy street. The world truly had gone to shit, but his tiny part of the mighty green machine was still operating.

It won't be for long, though, he thought to himself with a growing feeling of dread, *not unless I can get these people somewhere else and soon.*

Trusting his sergeants had been the right thing to do, as the tactics had been adapted overnight to dismount each crew with the exception of a single gunner, then use those dismounted troopers to constantly patrol the perimeter of their secure section. This had kept the initial crowd off the fences. From the reports he had received and the intelligence he had first hand, he believed that the only threat to their immediate safety lay in the faster ones who could apparently climb the fence, or enough of the shambling Screechers showing up so that they could collapse the fence.

He exchanged a few words with the duty troop sergeant, recognised that his presence was not needed, and left to return to the command centre.

Walking in, he startled a Corporal, who turned with two full tin mugs of steaming tea and jumped as he did not expect anyone to be there, let alone his ranking leader. Recovering, he seemed to hesitate as he furrowed his brow, and started to hold out one mug to the SSM, then retracted it and offered the other, then shook his head and offered him the first one again with a smile.

Taking it with one hand and offering the Corporal his Sterling sub-machine gun in exchange, he sipped the too-hot tea and nodded at its strong, starchy flavour and sweetness of the added sugar.

"Where are we, gentlemen?" he asked the room loudly.

"Sir," Corporal Daniels said from under a radio headset, "Yeovilton have got back to us, they are reporting mass movement of enemy all over the south east, and their Marines on-base have had engagements."

"You've passed on everything we know about the fast ones? The Leaders?" the SSM asked him.

"Yes, and they've reported that they are planning a withdrawal by air if necessary to the south west and then onto naval vessels," Daniels answered.

"Ah," Johnson said out loud and instantly regretted pulling back the curtain on his thoughts through tiredness, "can they extract our civilian population?"

Daniels turned back to the radio to have the exchange necessary to get that answer, as Johnson turned to a Lance Corporal who was poring over a large-scale map of the area they occupied. They all knew that area well, as, they lived within a sensible distance. Moreover, they had spent numerous weekends practising their vehicle patrol drills in the urban training areas as well as the large, open landscape of the windswept cliffs above the English Channel, where their live fire exercises were conducted.

Johnson, keeping his immediate fears to himself, looked at that familiar section of coast portrayed on paper and forced himself to decide. That decision came only moments later, but he knew that any decision arrived at so quickly was merely the very bones of an idea. It was a concept, not a plan. A plan, he knew, required other brains able to see the problem and the solution in a different light. Deciding to use those brains now, he sipped his tea and cleared his throat for attention.

"Gather round, chaps," he said, hearing another cough for attention at the doorway and seeing Sergeant Maxwell hovering for permission to enter.

"Come in, Simon," the SSM said genially, before addressing the assembly. The air in the room hung heavy, and that seemed to make their combined cigarette smoke linger above the dimly-lit central desk where the map was laid flat, which gave their meeting an air of an illicit gambling den, or a French Resistance meeting during the Second World War.

"Our problem," he began, "is that our current location is not viable in the long term," he said, pausing to let that fact sink in, "so we need an alternative. Today."

Silence hung for a few seconds before Maxwell offered his opinion. As the sergeant in charge of the assault and reconnaissance troop of the squadron, he was a man everyone knew, and his opinion was almost always worth listening to, unless it was on the subject of music, as the only cassette he owned was by Kenny Rogers.

"It's not a case of looking for a traditional spot for our cars," he explained, "because our enemy doesn't use armour or artillery. We need somewhere that we can block off and hold, like a high wall or one way in and out," he paused, scanning his eyes down the coastline until he evidently found the place that Johnson was already sizing up. "There," he said as he stabbed a finger onto the map."

"The island?" the tea-making soldier asked.

"It's connected by a causeway," Johnson said, "one heavy road bridge over fast-flowing water. Low ground to the immediate front, high cliffs rising either side of that. Low water for access to sea-faring craft, and enough of an infrastructure to keep us equipped until we are resupplied."

The others listened to him in silence, making him wish that he had kept his opinion to himself until the others had spoken.

Usually, he would offer his thoughts and then the Captain and the Major would consider alternatives, but without them present, nobody wanted to seem as though they were disagreeing with the SSM.

Having stopped the discussion unintentionally, he now asked them to come up with alternatives as their task, as though the decision to occupy and fortify a small island immediately off the coast wasn't a done deal.

"No," said another Corporal from the HQ troop, "I like it. Take the barriers off the side of the road bridge and barricade it with a wedge, and that way, anything like the crowds that came at us last night would go straight in the drink."

"Air assets?" another asked. "Is there room for a bird to land up there?"

"The top of the island, by the lighthouse. You could land a Chinook there, although more than one might be a stretch," offered the Corporal.

"And we're assuming that the disease hasn't affected the population yet?" Maxwell asked.

"It's further west than we are, and a bit out of the way," another said, "they might have been lucky."

Just then, Daniels called the SSM by name.

"What is it?" he asked, waiting for the response from the Navy pilots.

"They've asked where they are supposed to take them," he explained. "They are operating under the impression that the country is going to be overrun very soon. They are flying pilots *in* so that they can get enough of their air assets *out* of the base before they are overrun themselves."

Johnson resisted the urge to swear and give his opinion of the Fleet Air Arm, and instead, calmly requested the loan of a single rotary wing for reconnaissance and transport. The request was recited, the pause as it was contemplated was long, and the response was simple. They couldn't guarantee it, but they would allocate an asset if and when one became available.

The silence that this news left in the room didn't last long, because it was shattered by shouts from outside as the troop radio crackled into noisy life. The only thing louder than the shouts, louder than the unmistakable reports of multiple calibres of gunfire, was the massed chorus of screeching.

~

Just as the clean-up operation was being organised, the few irregular stragglers dispatched as soon as they stumbled close enough, shouts of alarm rippled along the section of fence to the right of the gate. Those shouts, ill-disciplined given that their new enemy operated on sound to acquire their location, spread panic. That panic, however, was both understandable and justified.

From what Strauss and his troop had seen the previous day, the Screechers seemed to have their own rudimentary rank structure. Most of them that the troop had encountered were the hissing, moaning, shuffling ones that moved like a drunk with slightly better balance.

However, they seemed to group up into roughly the size of an infantry company under the guidance of one of the god-awful ones that the soldiers had started to call Leaders, who seemed to have retained a little more of the motor functions of a living human. They were coordinated enough to run and, evidently from the attack on the camp in the night, climb. For each of those, came their followers of a hundred or so shuffling monsters, and when they reached sight of the men working at the fence line, the Leaders let out their piercing shrieks and broke into a run. Not only did that whip up the other Screechers into a slower-moving frenzy, but it sparked the faster ones themselves into a kind of bloodlust which made them moderately hard to kill.

By the time the troopers had been made aware of the incoming threat, and organised themselves to defend against it, the Leaders were at the wire and scaling it. The echoing, gassy reports of the troopers' Sterlings were punctuated by the far harsher reports of the SLRs, the heavy-calibre Self Loading Rifles belonging to the RMPs at the gate. Only when that first ragged volley had cut down the three leaping corpses with their pink-foamed mouths hanging open in death through a combination of frothing saliva and blood, did the troopers switch on to the danger that close to three hundred Screechers were almost at the wire.

The noise that came from those three hundred mouths was directly from the worst horror film ever made. A few troopers even dropped their weapons to cover their ears, such was the painful volume it reached. The three crowds converged where their Leaders had fallen, all combining to become a single, feverish, screeching, roiling mass of flesh and teeth. The smell from those bodies even at a distance was sufficient to bring tears to their eyes, and the only way to render that threat safe was to do what they knew how to do best.

The orders were given by hand signal, and the cupola of one Fox and one Spartan turned towards the crowd, and both gunners let rip.

There were twenty troopers and soldiers at the fence, so the crews in the armoured cars sensibly drove to the flanks, where they could bring their weapons to bear without risk of hitting their own side. When those guns sparked into life, the odds rapidly swung in favour of the living over the dead.

Both fired their GPMGs, the Spartan as it was the tank's only weapon and the Fox as its secondary, coaxial gun. The two heavy machine guns, combined with small arms fire from the front, tore ragged and bloody swathes into the hungry mob. The gunner of the Fox, eager to employ his instrument of warfare to its fullest, then fired six quick shots through the 30mm Rarden cannon, as the barrel was traversed ever so slightly after each shot.

The result of this, the 30mm coming somewhere between an extremely heavy machine gun and small artillery, was brutal, devastating and utterly awesome.

As the six shells rocketed through the crowd in a slow-moving arc, each heavy piece tore down dozens of bodies and pulped anything it hit into instant, bloody ruin. The guns were designed to fire ammunition that would kill Russian tanks, not for crowd control.

After those six shots, the gunner went back to intermittent fire on the coaxial GPMG, as there was little or no concentration of enemy remaining. The guns on the cars stopped, leaving the dismounted troopers to finish off anything that still moved with any kind of purpose.

"Cease fire," Johnson bawled as he approached the gate at a steady run, "cease fire."

What he saw when he got there could best be described as horrific. It was total and utter slaughterhouse carnage. It was a scene out of the deepest, darkest layers of hell. Stopping at the steaming, writhing pile of meat fanning out from where they had converged on the fence, he found himself locked into the stare of a pair of blind eyes as the creature's right hand reached for him. The left hand was gone, along with that shoulder, and a diagonal line out of the torso culminating in a pile of oily intestines sat atop the severed legs which he couldn't be certain even belonged to that particular Screecher. It opened its mouth as it craned towards him, hoping to cover the distance and somehow get through the chain link by sheer effort of will.

Turning away, Johnson locked eyes instead with the next man to catch up with him, Sergeant Maxwell.

"That settles it then," he said, "we head for the island as soon as we are able to move."

Watching him walk away, no doubt to give the necessary order or to assure the civilians that they were safe, Maxwell turned around and looked down at the horror that was a quarter of a human being still trying to eat him, even though it no longer possessed enough of its body to locomote. Ignoring the good sense that he should save his ammunition or that the thing was no longer a threat, he raised his gun and fired a single bullet into its skull to end the hunger for good.

~

"What's going on?" shouted a woman as she fussed to keep her hands over the ears of two children.

Kimberley also wanted, very much in fact, to know what was going on. The sergeant who had initially led them though to this large room, and who had organised two men to bring them a large rucksack containing a sleeping bag and some metal cooking tins, was standing at the doors, guarding them from going outside no doubt, and she knew he wouldn't tell her a thing. She decided to approach the new man they had just been introduced to and pulled her hair down the left side of her face to hide the scars as best she could.

Straightening herself to use her above average height to her advantage, she smoothed down her creased clothes and walked confidently towards the soldier who, she guessed, was about her age.

"Excuse me," she said, tapping him lightly on the shoulder and smiling as he turned around to face her, meeting the level of her eyes exactly. He returned the smile warmly, as though proper manners came easily to him, and those manners were so impeccable that when his eyes caught sight of the small patch of scar she could not obscure with her hair, his face did not register any disgust or flinch, merely switched back to her gaze and fixed her to the spot. One corner of his mouth curled up slightly, and he offered a hint of a bow to her.

"Madam," he said in a richly cultured accent, or at least an accent that others might find cultured, as Kimberley thought it made him sound like a smarmy dick.

"Lieutenant Oliver Simpkins-Palmer," he said, giving his full title in an attempt to make himself sound grand and important. He clearly had misjudged his audience, as Kimberley found herself in the unexpected role reversal of being repulsed by another person on sight.

"Kimberley Perkins," she answered curtly, unable to bring herself to be rude despite instantly disliking the man in front of her. "Lieutenant, might I enquire as to what is going on, and how long we are to be kept here?"

"My dear Miss Perkins," he crooned like some awful approximation of a character in an Ian Fleming novel, "if everyone can remain inside and let the chaps handle things, then all will be well, I assure you," he continued, offering her another dazzling smile.

"I'm sure you're right," she responded, "but that answers neither of my questions."

Palmer's smile barely quivered before he brought it back under control.

"Madam, again I assure you that everything is under control, and everyone here," she winced as he pronounced the word as *hy'ah* directly from his sinuses, "will be brought up to speed very shortly. Now, if you'll excuse me?" he said, clearly desperate to find someone not immune to his upper-class charm.

Kimberley was left standing alone and even more annoyed than before. Something inside her said that she needed to be ready to move and soon, so she returned to the space where she had slept in her new, thick green sleeping bag and rolled it back up to stuff it into her new army backpack to keep the metal tins from rattling around. Settling the large bag over one shoulder, she took herself to the long table that contained military clothing, because the skirt and heels were unlikely to be fitting for any kind of flight from the base which she sensed would be coming at some point. Taking a bundle, after searching the piles for labels, she retired to the toilets designated for female use.

She found a pair of green trousers that fit over her hips but weren't quite long enough to reach all the way down the length of her legs. She countered this with a pair of boots, the tops of which covered the trouser legs. They were half a size too large for her, but laced up tight enough, she kept her feet from slipping. Abandoning her skirt, blouse, tights and heels, which went into her bag, she completed her new look with a white T-shirt with red hemming around the neck and sleeves. The only outer garment she could find was a smock, a kind of large blouse jacket, of stiff camouflage-patterned material which was at least three sizes too big for her. She also kept another pair of trousers and a few T-shirts, which she stuffed into the bag.

When she returned to the main hall and propped her army luggage on a chair, she fetched one or two strange looks from the frightened people who were just cowering there waiting to be told what to do, and she helped herself to the stewed coffee from the pot which was permanently kept warm on a cycle. She was certain that the amount of coffee she was drinking couldn't be good for her, but she doubted that the sudden influx of so much caffeine in her life would lead to her imminent demise, as she rather expected that to be something terrifyingly similar to what she had seen back in the town where she lived.

Used to live, she corrected herself, *can't see that place being habitable any time soon.*

Within twenty minutes, her predictions became reality when she saw entering the room a very stressed looking man with stripes on his arm and his hair tousled on one side, carrying a battered clipboard. He loudly announced that everyone needed to be ready to go very soon, then left the room under a barrage of shouted questions, with the young officer following.

Smiling to herself, Kimberley watched as everyone scrabbled to grab clothing and throw things into their bags. ready to leave.

Chapter 21

Peter, who had decided that his task for the morning was to climb a particularly tall oak tree, heard what he thought was thunder rolling over the undulating ground towards him. An experienced solider would have recognised it as gunfire, heavy gunfire at that, but Peter had no way of knowing. He had heard something very similar, only lasting longer, a few times the previous day, only from further away.

Now, close to forty feet from the ground, he stood shakily to hold onto a swaying branch as he scanned the landscape in a roughly two-hundred-and-seventy-degree arc. He saw nothing, except the few farm buildings, the three houses of the Pines, the scary mansion further up the lane and the road itself in parts. Nothing moved, except for wildlife and the cows and pigs in the field below. Looking as far as he could see in the other direction, his brain did not register the brick building with its outbuildings and detached garage.

He was so high up that he really could see his house from there, only that house no longer existed in his mind.

After watching for long enough that his legs began to feel wobbly through a combination of tiredness and vertigo, he carefully monkeyed his way down to ground level, and dangled to endure the last drop from a branch the height of a full-grown man.

Picking himself up out of the leaf mould, he brushed himself down and retrieved his bag and weapons which went everywhere with him, with the exception of the shotgun which he now intended to deal with.

Had he been able to see through the higher branches and leaves of the tree, had he been able to look in the direction of the pub and the shop and eventually behind that to the town, then he would have been able to see the dark line smearing over the horizon where the dead had amassed and turned their faces towards the sound of the distant, rolling gunfire. Beginning their nearly thirty-mile cross country journey towards the source of their excitement, they began to trudge on a course that would lead them straight through the farm.

Peter, totally unaware that by that afternoon the farm would be washed away by a tidal wave of dead, opened up the workshop again and went about some very illegal weapon modifications. First, choosing the hardest task to begin with, he broke down the gun and clamped the barrels into the vice, where he took the same hacksaw from the white wall and exposed the silhouette of the tool in black pen once more. Repeating the skills he had been grudgingly taught, he dragged the blade back towards him across the metal, planning to remove two-thirds of the length.

That took him close to an hour, as he had to stop for frequent breaks and twice to replace blunted and broken saw blades. When he had finally taken off the section, he spent a further twenty minutes making sure that the ends were smoothed down, using the file again. That done, he turned his attention to the stock of the weapon and used another hand saw to take the shoulder stock off at the handle, effectively making the weapon one huge, double-barrelled pistol. Using a rasp file, he shaped the wood, intermittently placing his hand around the grip to see where he needed to reduce the profile to best fit him. When that was finally done, he used gradually finer grades of sandpaper to finish the wood and thanked the state school curriculum for insisting that design and technology be taught. Making things with his hands gave Peter a sense of achievement in a life generally devoid of success or happiness.

Snapping the three parts of the gun back together, Peter turned his attention to the ammunition. This was a rare and illegal skill which his father had taught him, on one of those occasions where he coincidentally enjoyed something he was forced to do, so didn't realise it wasn't being done for his benefit. Removing each cartridge from the belt, he placed them on the workbench and used the folding pen knife he had taken from his father's bedside table to prise open the crimped plastic ends.

Having used a match from the box of long fire-lighting matches taken from the house that no longer existed to him, he lit three candles after he had finished opening each red shotgun cartridge, to leave them standing in a row with their brown wading exposed to the air.

Lifting up that wadding each time with the tip of the knife, he poured in the dripping wax with painstakingly slow progress, until only three stubs of wax remained alight and his back ached from leaning over the bench for so long. Closing down the flared ends of the cartridges, he pressed them flat and added a small strip of green and yellow striped electrical earth tape to ensure the solid ball of wax and lead stayed inside until such time as it was needed. Restoring the cartridges to the belt, he loaded two and played around with how best to hold and carry the gun, deciding on cutting a small hole into his bag so that the barrels pointed down his back.

~

"Quartermaster, where are we with those Bedfords for the civilians?" Johnson barked, not having the luxury of time to address the second highest ranking NCO in their squadron with the proper courtesies.

In simple response, Staff Sergeant Rochefort held up both hands with all the digits splayed out after tucking the thing he was carrying under one arm.

Luckily, most of the supplies they had brought with them were still stowed on the trucks, but they had not had sufficient time to organise the unloading of stores on the base to a sufficient degree to consider abandoning it. Now they had less than an hour to get those supplies loaded again, and all the while more and more of the things were approaching the gate. Very few came from any other directions, but logic suggested the reason for this was that the gate pointed directly towards town in an easterly direction. Behind them was the tank proving grounds, where not too many of the local population chose to reside.

The situation at the gate was beginning to cause some alarm, and Johnson thought for ten long seconds before snapping out of his torpor and ordering a bold move.

"Sergeant Maxwell?" he boomed over the sounds of engines and the occasional gunshot.

"Here," Maxwell responded from behind him.

"Take your troop out, if you'll oblige me, head towards town, shooting intermittently, draw them away from here and take a longer route back round to the island. Can you have one of your chaps map it?" he asked, eyes wide with expectation and hope that Maxwell would get it done, and get it done right.

He nodded, telling the SSM that he'd get it mapped en route, and called for his troop to mount their Spartans.

Within minutes, the four tracked vehicles rattled and squeaked their way noisily out of the gate and down the road, where their cupola-mounted GPMGs barked sporadically to fire bursts of heavy 7.62mm into any Screecher that showed itself in the open. As their thunderous noise faded away, so did the intensity of the enemy encroachment as their attention was taken up by the moving sound generators that was the squadron's reconnaissance screen of light armour.

With the imminent risk reduced tenfold, Johnson was able to leave a single fighting troop on point duty at any one time, and to organise the others into ensuring that everything they needed was getting loaded somewhere. All of the admin troop now had their own Bedford four-tonne truck, which was being loaded with a combination of food, other supplies, ammunition, fuel jerrycans, not to mention to close to sixty civilians who had either been rescued, or who had trickled in after the squadron had been able to let people know to leave their homes immediately.

Not that their current predicament was much better than being in their own homes.

Fuel had been pumped into mobile tankers, the kind that resupplied them on the battlefield, and they had finally taken as much as they could carry. Calling for the civilians to be loaded into the Bedford trucks alongside whatever supplies were already on board, Johnson mounted his own armoured vehicle and kept his head above the hatch with his hand on the machine gun.

Their convoy, now twenty-two vehicles long and comprising twelve Foxes, one Sultan and nine of the big, green Bedford trucks, was not an easy thing to manage. For starters, they spread out to over a quarter of a mile in length from nose to tail and the interspersing of fighting units between the soft-skinned vehicles meant that very quickly their troop unit cohesion evaporated. Johnson was at the lead, or behind two Foxes of Two Troop, and he had placed Strauss' entire troop at the rear, with the six remaining cars of Two and Three Troops mixed throughout the convoy to provide a screen, should they encounter enemy anywhere other than their front or rear.

As they drove away, their progress was slow, because although even the tracked vehicle of Johnson's was the slowest of them with a top speed only just north of fifty, the constant stopping to wait as the trucks and cars ahead manoeuvred, made them bunch up tight and remain stationary for long periods of time. Stationary vehicles, especially the soft-skinned trucks with no armour to hide behind, were a concern for Johnson. In conventional warfare, not that he should keep drawing parallels, such a concertina effect on a large convoy would be fatal as their entire force could be eradicated with a single artillery barrage or airstrike. He kicked himself for making that irrelevant distinction, as he was fairly certain that no corpse could operate instruments of war. Even if some of them could climb fences.

The net result of their halting progress was an average speed close to about ten miles per hour. Given that the island was over thirty miles from their position, that progress was painfully slow and frustrating for all of them, and the SSM's distracted thoughts were snatched back to the inside of his car by Corporal Daniels.

"Sir, getting something on the Clansman," he said, gesturing at one of the two radio sets in the relatively spacious interior for an armoured vehicle. Johnson let his hand slip away from the machine gun and dropped back inside.

"What is it?" he asked.

"Not sure," Daniels said loudly with a frown, "intermittent and broken, but definitely not one of ours; they've all reported in when called."

It was Johnson's turn to frown. What other military units could be calling up in this area? There was almost nothing between their area and the Navy bases in the south west, certainly nothing green army, but his contemplation was ceased by Daniels answering another radio hail.

"Foxtrot-Three-Three-Alpha receiving," he said in that implacable tone of voice that born radio operators possessed, before pausing to listen to the response. "It's Sarn't Maxwell, he's reached the island and is holding firm on the road bridge…" he paused to listen again, "low concentration of enemy… no Screechers coming from the island towards their noise."

"Good," Johnson growled, "tell him to push inland one mile and secure some higher ground. Tell him we are," he looked at his watch and glanced to the map on the inside wall of the hull to gauge their speed and distance, "ninety minutes away at least."

Daniels nodded and turned to his radio sets to relay the information, then Johnson paused as he went to raise himself up and out of the hatch again, as the Corporal switched dials on the radio sets and spoke intently.

"Last callsign, repeat, I say again, repeat," he said, giving their squadron callsign and disposition briefly, then stayed still and silent waiting for a response which must have come through garbled, because he repeated his last transmission word for word before waiting again. Giving up he shook his head and went back to the switches and dials.

~

Feeling satisfied with himself, Peter's little bubble of happiness was burst by the sudden rise in noises from the farm. He had always been accustomed to the sounds of cattle and other livestock, but the tone and desperation of the noises coming from the cows made his chest feel tight and cold. Running out of his barn and skidding to a stop to turn and run back inside, he snatched up the camouflage backpack that he knew must go everywhere with him and must always be packed ready.

In that bag he had snacks, a canteen of water, his sleeping back and the stuffed lamb belonging at one time to his sister, and the belt of ammunition for the shotgun, because it was too big to fit around his slim waist. The folding penknife never left his pocket unless he was using it, so he was ready to go as soon as he snatched up his pitchfork.

Rounding the corner of a building, he couldn't help but gasp out loud as the sight that greeted him was worse than anything he could have imagined.

It had started somewhere miles away, and as each new addition to the group was drawn towards the sound and movement of the others, so too were they all tugged inexorably towards the sounds in the distance. Those ripples of rolling thunder made the few more alert ones of them sniff the air in that direction and move, dragging the slower ones on with them, as if they were being towed. Every infected corpse they passed reacted to the presence of the growing crowd of dead, and the cycle continued as more and more of them added to the noise, which drew yet more in from areas unaffected by the direct path they took.

Those who had been almost dormant from the lack of noise or movement to spark their feeding instincts, suddenly came alive with renewed intensity to join the hunt, as hundreds of them moved together and none of them could know where they were going or why.

Their direct path took them through the woodland and the shallow river into a farm, where things started moving and making noises. The Leaders at the front, half a dozen of them, sniffed greedily at the air and went into a frenzy as the smell of flesh excited them. They threw themselves forwards, some leaping the chest-high fence entirely, and fell upon the innocent cattle mercilessly. Their pitiful bellows tore the air as teeth chewed through thick skin and blood flowed in thick globules down to the dry dirt, where it soaked in to make a dark red mud that the following zombies trampled into unthinkingly. They too now had their arms reaching out, and their mouths opened wide to peel back their lips and show teeth as they saw flesh. The wooden fence, a simple and strong enough barrier, splintered like toothpicks under the combined crushing weight of hundreds of bodies, some of whom went down with the obstacle to be trampled flat by their careless comrades.

The cows stood no chance and were all pulled to the ground and devoured. One lumbering beast, her eyes wide in terror at the stench of blood, kicked out and scored a lucky hit on one attacker to crush its skull and drop it lifeless to the wet dirt, but the temporary reprieve did little for her long-term survival, and the next one in line simply took the place of the ruined skull and bit down hard.

Peter, rounding the corner to see this emerging carnage, could luckily not be heard over the terrible noise, but something made two of them turn towards him.

Perhaps his smell, perhaps some other sense, but two of them had locked on to him and began to move his way.

He forced his feet to respond to the messages his brain was sending desperately, finally getting them to stumble him backwards. A third zombie, eyes cloudy and pale and the white shirt under his grey suit a mess of both fresh and dried blood, burst from the mass and also went after him, but this one did so with more coordination and at a much faster pace.

Peter ran. He ran as fast as he physically could. He ran faster than he ever had before, even when he was unencumbered by a heavy bag, a sawn-off shotgun and an awkward pitchfork in one hand. Hearing the sound of footsteps approaching behind him even over the rasping of his own breathing and the blood pumping through his ears deafeningly, he instinctively turned to his right to fall through an open stable doorway. The thing chasing him shot past and fell hard to the concrete yard, making a sound like meat hitting a chopping board, and Peter managed to kick the door closed behind. The man in the suit had already got to his feet and banged hard into the half door, reaching over and down to try and grab Peter. He thrust forward with his pitchfork, skewering the man straight through the throat and having no effect whatsoever to stop him.

The end of the weapon's handle slipped from his grasp and flung around to hit him on the head twice.

His own screams of fear mixed with the screeching, hissing noise the thing made as it leaned further over at him. The pitchfork prevented the man in the suit from getting to him, as the end wedged tight against the pitted ground and held his head upright.

Which gave Peter just enough time to reach high above his head and grasp the newly-smoothed handle of the shotgun. Unthinking, he pulled it free, aimed it upwards and pushed the safety catch off with his thumb. Reaching his small index finger forwards to reach one of the triggers, he snatched at the thin metal.

The responding boom of the gun going off inside the confined space was huge. He was blinded temporarily, deafened and left in total shock by the savagery of the report. The gun had flown backwards as it fired, slamming the barrel back into his shoulder, where the padded strap luckily prevented any serious injury.

Before his vision went white from the blast, he was left with a brief snapshot of the suit man's head vanishing. The headless body flopped over the stable door, and Peter took three ragged breaths before his survival instinct kicked in again. Part of him knew that the noise would bring more, that he had to run and hide, and that part of him dragged him to his feet and forced him to pick up the discarded pitchfork. Pushing open the half door with difficulty as the headless body was partly obstructing it, he ran just as four reaching hands grabbed at his clothing.

He had no idea how many were chasing him, but one was one too many. He tore blindly through the collection of mismatched buildings until he lost his footing and fell headlong to the hard ground, where he slid without slowing down.

What he slid through was ankle-deep animal shit. It got in his face and forced him to close his eyes. It got in his mouth and he turned his face away, which caused the slimy filth to collect in his right ear and deafen him on that side. Skidding to a stop he retched and shuddered, spitting out the disgusting contents of his mouth. He rolled sideways to try and escape his pursuit by cramming himself under the small section of air between the rough ground and the raised floor of a building. Reaching to his waist he managed to free the canteen of water which he poured on his face to swill his mouth and stop him from vomiting.

As his wits were restored to him, he noticed feet about three paces from his face just at the edge of the building. He froze, not wanting or daring to move or breathe, just hoping that they would go away.

Then he remembered the way they sniffed the air.

He could hear them snuffling, knowing that something they could eat had gone this way and disappeared, trying to detect it through smell. But they couldn't. Peter stayed exactly where he was, not daring to move in case he made a sound or changed his smell in some way.

He rested his head slowly to the ground, slowed his breathing, and watched as feet after feet traipsed past him. He lost count of how many in the first few seconds, and only a few details remained in his mind. Like the size of some of the feet being smaller than his own, or the red high-heeled shoes with both heels snapped off making the already jerky movements seem even more ungainly.

Peter stayed there until the herd had become a trickle and stayed still even when that trickle had faded to nothing. When the sun first began to set, he tentatively crawled out from under the building and raised his pitchfork to sweep the area for any stragglers that had got left behind. Creeping out from behind the building, he let out a strangled cry and felt his knees give from underneath him. He fell down, cracking the film of dried shit from his skin and refreshing the smell. The scene before him was horrific, even worse than the torn mess of the dog he had tried to tell himself he hadn't seen.

The big, docile and harmless creatures had been ravaged and torn apart to be left in ruin where they fell. The flesh had been flensed from their bones, leaving great arcs of white bones from the ribcages. At the sound he made, a gargling, bubbling groan escaped from the far side of one of the poor, dead cows. One of the things, slow-moving and fat-faced with wobbling jowls, rose awkwardly to its feet and began to hobble towards him. It was slow because of its weight, and the fact that one of its feet was turned to face backwards and made a sickening crunching noise as it moved.

Just as the bones in the ankle of the fat creature had gone, something inside Peter snapped then.

He straightened, twirled the pitchfork, then stepped towards it and ran the two spikes through its eyes to burst straight out the back of its skull. It fell backwards like a tree and he let the weapon go for it to bounce out of the skull when it impacted the ground with a slap. He stepped over, picked up his weapons and, for the first time in his life, listened to the total absence of sound as every animal on the farm was dead.

And he could not stay there one minute longer.

Chapter 22

Eight vehicles from the front of the convoy, Kimberley tried to ignore the cramp and the discomfort of travelling in the back of a very industrial truck. It was not designed for comfort, but then again everything she had seen in the last couple of days indicated that Her Majesty's Armed Forces, or the army at least, did not rate personal comfort high on their agenda. Finally, unable to suffer the annoyance of her loose hair bouncing into her face with every lurching turn or juddering gear change, she tied it back into a ponytail and thanked the gloomy interior for obscuring that part of her face that she had kept covered for the last three years whenever there were other people around her. The journey seemed to take forever, with the truck constantly halting to a stop amidst the protesting shriek of brake pads. The first few times the brakes had made that high-pitched sound after they had warmed had made her heart lurch into her stomach and her eyes grow wide with the adrenaline that forced her breathing to speed up. Realising that the screech was of brakes and not torn from the throat of a flesh-eating and insane former person, she relaxed and each time it happened she reacted less and less. Recognising that fear was debilitating her and having an effect on her body, she forced herself to remain calm through sheer will, and wait.

Just wait, she told herself from behind her eyelids, *everything ends eventually.*

~

"Unknown callsign this is Victor-Three-Zero identify yourself. Over," barked Daniels with more authority than before, confirm disposition."

"Hello Victor-Three-Zero, this is Delta-Two-Zero minus. We are a detached heavy callsign. Over."

Hearing the callsign he named, Johnson dropped back inside as though he had been shot and stared at the operator with eyes wider than the exhaust on a Chieftain tank, because that was precisely what he associated with that callsign.

His impatience almost killed him, but he did not let himself down by interrupting the exchange. Instead he waited until the necessary information had been exchanged and grid coordinates swapped. Calculating distance and speed very roughly in his head, Johnson reckoned that he had perhaps another hour before the slower moving units, realistically only able to move at half of their top speed, could combine with them.

"Give them our objective," he ordered Daniels, who nodded and relayed the information and then signed off.

"Two Chieftains," he said, confirming Johnson's hopes. "They were part of the armour sent to London, but they said they never got further than Southampton before they were swamped. Their Captain reckons th…"

"Their Captain?" he interrupted, betraying his own nervousness at his tenuous command of a squadron and fearing that he would be forced to relinquish control.

"Yes, Sir," Daniels said almost sympathetically, intuiting the cause of concern on his SSM's face, "he reckons they can be here in three hours, but they'll be very low on fuel by then."

"Replen?" Johnson asked, checking if it was necessary to send a resupply fuel wagon to meet them.

"Possibly," Daniels said as he thought, "when those things run low, their fuel filters get choked up and die," he mused, temporarily wearing his day job hat and thinking as a mechanic. "Let's see what we have at the island and then decide?"

Johnson nodded to agree to the logical course of action, then turned his attention back to their route ahead and tried to push away the nagging sense of self-doubt as he prepared to justify his orders to a senior officer.

Second Lieutenant Oliver Simpkins-Bloody-Palmer was too junior to test an NCO of his experience, but a Captain in an armoured division would be far more likely to have something other than fine lace and dance steps between his ears.

That introspection lasted until his scanning eyes rested on the long, straight approach road leading to the lump of rock just off the coast.

That rock, not that he yet knew it, would soon become the most contested piece of land in many miles.

~

"Sir?" the driver of the lead tank said into the microphone on his headset to get the attention of their Captain.

"Everything ok, Wells?" the officer asked in genuine concern as he peered forward to where their Lance Corporal was enduring the awkward driving position forced on him by being closed down. Closed down was the term for having their hatches firmly secured, and it was the only reason they all still lived.

"She's juddering, Sir," Clive Wells answered from his seat at the front which required him to be lying almost flat on his back, "under throttle. She doesn't like something."

The Captain frowned, rechecked their position on the map in the cramped confines, and called for a full stop to his crew's loader, who also acted as radio operator, which he relayed over the group radio. The second tank, with her complement of four, also ground to a halt behind them for their roaring engines to drop to a low rumble at idle. Checking all around, the Captain opened up the hatch to climb out and converse with the other crew, commanded by a Sergeant named Horton.

"We're starting to get engine problems," the officer explained.

"We aren't much better off, Sir," the sergeant responded in a voice laced with angry disappointment. "We've lost our gears and are on emergency ones."

Both of their wagons, the only surviving armour from their massed foray to rescue the capital, were splattered with dried gore and were less than fresh on the inside too. They had barely felt safe enough to open the hatches in days for more than a few minutes at a time because the creatures would emerge to clamber up their low hulls and claw at the closed hatches. Because their tanks weren't that fast moving, getting one of them stuck on the top was best avoided. They had all seen what had happened to the other armour in their column, not to mention the occupants of the soft-skinned and canvas-backed vehicles, when they had stopped moving and were overrun by the crowds.

There were two reasons why their pair of green and black painted tanks had escaped from that swarm of bodies. One was partly down to luck in that they had stopped to inspect a minor repair, and as no tank would be left alone the pair arrived at the very tail end of the halted convoy. The other was down to the very quick thinking of the officer who had been thrown into their crew at the very last minute, the column having been formed in a hurry. He had presence which gave his orders an authority which prompted instant obedience in the men. He had ordered them to close down and reverse, which they did, and now they had survived and not been overrun or stranded on mounds of bodies.

Hearing and then seeing a pair of jets overhead as they reversed their course made them try a hail, which eventually got them in touch with a large Naval air station. They, in turn, advised them of army units active at the place where their own journey had begun, so they made to return there. Attempting at regular intervals on their slow journey to raise the base, they eventually made contact and altered course to head for the spit of high ground separated from the mainland by a causeway bridge. The Captain knew the area to be a small town, more of a village really, with some farming and a lighthouse. Given their unexpected predicament, the choice of location made instant sense to him and he made a note to congratulate the man who came up with the idea. His own wagon, named Annabelle by the men of A Squadron, was fitted with the heavy plough that they had anticipated needing for clearing abandoned vehicles out of the city streets. That had been useful when needing to clear the way of lumbering corpses, but it added weight to them and ultimately reduced their speed and increased their fuel consumption.

"Confirm our location," the Captain said to his radio man, "contact that armoured unit and request a resupply of fuel. Vehicle mechanics too, if they have any, because I'd rather like to keep these two ladies in the fight."

The man nodded, enthused by the short speech and infectious good nature of the man who was not his officer, but had quickly proven himself to be one of the best.

Still a young man, as well-bred Captains often were, he seemed to possess a depth of character that lent him the air of an older man.

The Captain hefted his gun and invited Sergeant Horton to join him on stag to protect their crews.

~

"Sarn't Major?" Daniels called out to bring Johnson back to the Sultan.

"Yes?"

"It's the armour, Sir," he explained, "I've got grid co-ords for them, but they are stranded, requesting replen and vehicle mechs if we have them."

Johnson had no REME, no men of the Royal Electrical and Mechanical Engineers or other army mechanics to deploy, but he was certain that he could fix the issue himself. Kicking that thought aside, as much as he would have loved to go and perform a battlefield repair and get his hands dirty, he was forced to attend to the more pressing matters.

"Ask Strauss if he's up to it," Johnson told the radio man, knowing that the sergeant was both a steady leader and had a few half-decent mechanics in his troop, "and if he is, he should top off his tanks and go now."

Now that he thought about it, given their vehicles' inclinations towards mechanical failure, he reckoned that most of his squadron were half-decent mechanics by that point.

Turning his attention back to the long, straight stretch of road leading directly to the island, Johnson raised the binoculars he had borrowed from a trooper in Three Troop and scanned the small town on their rock.

What he saw made him laugh. He dropped the binoculars in disbelief, raised them again and let out another involuntary chuckle at the sight. Keeping them in focus and finding yet another thing to amuse him, he could no longer contain himself and he burst out in almost uncontrollable belly laughs. All around him troopers and NCOs exchanged awkward looks of fear as their senior man had finally lost the plot and spilled whatever was left of his marbles all over the road.

"They're…" he giggled as he wiped a tear away from his eye, "they're…"

"Good God, man," snapped Lieutenant Palmer incredulously, "what's got into you? Pull yourself together!"

Still laughing, Johnson passed the binoculars roughly into Palmer's chest. Puzzled, he looked through them for the source of the hilarity and soon found it.

"Oh," he exclaimed, "oh my word, whatever do they…" he broke off to giggle, "I say, do they think we're…?"

He dropped the binoculars away from his face and joined the Sergeant Major in laughing until one of the troopers asked him what the joke was.

"Trooper," said Palmer in a high-pitched voice brought on by the humour, "the townsfolk are surrendering to us!"

It started with just one person who ran to the highest window in their house and threw it open to wave the white tablecloth into the wind. Others soon copied when the word had spread, and the people on the island looked down on a large column of tanks and other military vehicles which had stopped short of the town, and which were just looking up at them. Fearing some invading force, the townspeople had elected to show that they offered no resistance and hopefully avoid the bloodshed they feared.

"Lieutenant?" Johnson asked as he dried his eyes.

"Sarn't Major?" the young officer responded in the style of the men, which seemed to make him ever so slightly more human.

"Could you oblige me by letting the good folk of this town know that we are on their side, and aren't here to conquer them?"

Palmer bowed low in playful sarcasm to accept his task as though it were a dare on tour.

"Load up, boys," he said to the crew of the second Sultan as he skipped to climb up the tracks, "let's be the heroes, shall we? I say, does anyone have The Ride of the Valkyries to hand?" his rhetorical joke drew a smirk from the men and Johnson had the slight inkling that if the posh little twat survived long enough, he might actually learn to do some good.

Eventually.

"Maxwell," he said, turning to the man in charge of the four tracked vehicles of their reconnaissance assault troop, "push out a picquet line if you would, four hundred yards?"

Maxwell nodded his understanding, relishing getting back to one of his primary trained roles and acting as scouts for the heavier guns of their squadron. He shouted his orders, teased and cajoled his men into action. Johnson gave orders that left another four Fox wagons blocking the road with their guns set into defensive arcs, and sent all of the other fighting men and the HQ troop with their laden Bedford trucks up the hill into the town.

The SSM trusted Palmer, and he could not believe he actually used those words, to charm and pacify the frightened locals, and he also trusted the Squadron Quartermaster Sergeant to arrange the necessary accommodation and storage, and he trusted all of the men to ensure that none of the Screechers were on that island, as it was his job to make sure that the roadway stayed closed to their enemy.

It has been said that necessity is the mother of invention but, in Johnson's opinion, it was war. War made people come up with sudden inventions and ideas.

War made people find new ways of staying alive and new ways of killing others, and war made people as resourceful as MacGyver locked in a store cupboard full of innocuous items, taking them to build a rocket launcher.

Now, with no engineering team or necessary tools, he ordered the bridge cleared, and detailed the 30mm gunner on one Fox to destroy the parapet. The display was, they all had to admit, impressive. Using what they had in the limited time available, they formulated the fastest way to safely achieve what they needed to. They needed the parapets broken so that the road could be blockaded and anyone, any*thing*, pushing against the stop would fall off either side down into the fast-flowing current of the coast.

That was the theory, anyway, and any number of things could still go wrong.

Up in the town, Sergeant Croft had reported by radio that there was no infection, and that there was plenty of room for men, vehicles and equipment up there. The defences were simple, in the same way that medieval castle defences were simple. There was one way in, and they just had to kill anything that tried to use it. Johnson remained on the lower slopes of the island, watching over the troop of Fox vehicles, and using the binoculars to range further out into the distance to cover the two low hulls of the Spartans that he could see. He knew that the men out there, those he could and couldn't see, knew their jobs and were well led enough to not need his help, or interference, depending on how one looked at it.

His mind cast further out, away from the island they had successfully navigated to and begun to fortify, to where the five wagons he had sent were bumping along the tarmac towards the two silent hulks of armour and their massive 120mm guns. The Chieftain was, in Johnson's opinion, one of the finest instruments of warfare ever created. It was right up there with the Harrier jump jet. The only thing he would maybe have chosen to change, the small wrinkle in the silk for him, was the fact that the most reliable thing about the engines in those tanks was that they were guaranteed to break down regularly. Sending a troop out to refuel and help fix up two of the beasts was worth the risk on any day, and he was confident in Strauss' abilities. Already his mind's eye was planning for the added weight in defence in having the two tanks with them, even if it meant relinquishing his overall command to the Captain.

He thought on that, believing for a moment that he wouldn't mind that as long as he had confidence in this Captain to lead the men well, and a big part of him looked forward in happy anticipation to getting back to what he saw as his real job of running the squadron in its entirety, without being bogged down by the daily grind of making every command decision. Dragging his mind back, he looked out at the defences and knew that the plan had to be kept very simple.

The road was blocked, and the parapets would need tidying up for certain, and they could even try to rig a two- or even three-stage defence up at some point in the future, with outward-opening barriers that joined at an angle like a wedge to keep the Screechers out. Looking behind him, he saw only two shallow beaches where they could wash up randomly, and simple fencing could keep that issue at bay when combined with a quick reaction force on standby twenty-four hours a day and a morning search sweep. They would need to foray out for supplies and other survivors, obviously, but they could be safe there. He stayed there, assessing the approaches and vulnerabilities, until the time crept onwards and he began to worry about his absent soldiers.

Just then, his recce screen reported contact on the radio.

Chapter 23

"Sir, I hear armour coming," Wells warned the Captain in a low voice, who had heard the engine notes just as the man spoke.

"I hear them," he responded, "let's be ready, boys."

Their eyes were alert over their weapons, even more so given the increase in noise with the arrival of their resupply mission, and they had learned the hard lessons about bringing the bastards down on them by simply being too loud. The relief they felt, if not overtly shown, when the lead Fox bounced into view, was palpable. The lead car went straight up to them, with another going past and one driving off to the side, while the last about-turned and guarded the direction they had come from. The other vehicle with them was a fuel resupply one and drove in between the two silent tanks for maximum efficiency.

"Strauss, Yeomanry, C Squadron," said the tall sergeant as he held a hand out to the officer.

"Julian Simpkins-Palmer," the Captain responded, "Household Cavalry," then smiled hesitantly as the sergeant's face dropped and his features went slack in disbelief. Captain Palmer, as he went by for ease in the long tradition of the military men in his family, incorrectly suspected the source of the man's incredulity lay in the lack of the rest of the cavalry, and he offered a small shrug of apology.

"Best we could do in a tight spot, I'm afraid," he said, "still, can't imagine your Major would turn his nose up at a pair of these, eh?"

"No Sir," Strauss said, "we don't have a Major, Sir."

"Oh? Who is your Captain then? Perhaps I know the gentleman," Palmer tried, fearing that the man staring at him was being intentionally obtuse.

"Sir, my apologies," Strauss said, shaking himself out of the daze he was in and gesturing for the officer to walk with him. The sergeant produced a packet of cigarettes and offered one to the Captain, who surprised him by accepting one and producing his own lighter to put flame to the NCO's smoke before his own. Both men sucked in a lungful and exhaled slowly, then Strauss tried again.

"We are led by our SSM, Sir," he told him, seeing the mixed look of shock and distress on the Captain's face, "but we do have an officer…"

Just then the penny dropped.

"C Squadron?" Palmer asked, "You may have met my younger brother, he joined the reserves late last year," he said happily, then added, "but the little blighter had himself a weekend with the boys in London, that's why I jumped in with the first column headed that way, you see? Get things back under control."

"Sir," Strauss said, "your brother isn't in London…"

Palmer's face registered shock, then heart-warming happiness as though something he believed he had lost was found safely all along.

"You mean…?"

"Yes, Sir, he's with the squadron," Strauss told him. Palmer's eyes glazed slightly, and he insisted on shaking Strauss' hand again to thank him for the most welcome news.

"Sergeant Horton? Did you hear that?" he called over his shoulder as quietly as he could to prevent the noise carrying, although they were far more protected than they had been previously, "These fine fellows have my younger brother safe, he's a Lieutenant in the reserves."

Sergeant Horton smiled and nodded, then returned his face to the scowl it had been before he was spoken to. He didn't dislike the officer one bit, in fact he thought the man was bloody competent and owed him a lot for thinking fast and getting them out of there, it was more that he was busy trying to the get the two tanks refuelled and restarted so they could get the hell out of there, and he didn't think that some baby Rupert not being dead was worth the interruption.

The fuel was pumped and given a few minutes to settle into the engines before the ignition process was started, with elation and smiles all round as both beasts sparked to life at the first attempt. The convoy of now seven vehicles lumbered its way back at half the speed of the inbound journey, but then again none of the wagons that had made the outbound journey weighed close to fifty tonnes.

That wasn't strictly true, Horton allowed, as they weren't carrying all their really heavy sabot anti-armour artillery ammunition. Seeing as they had been deployed to show strength and restore the Queen's peace to the streets of London, they weren't issued with the tank-killers they carried whenever they were deployed in Germany, ready to head east at a moment's notice.

Feeling safer, given their slower progress and increased firepower, Strauss allowed himself the luxury of not being closed down on the return leg. He smoked a few cigarettes as they rolled on with Palmer's tank, called Annabelle, which made him smile in genuine happiness for some unknown reason, taking the lead. With the pace set by the first tank, the other wagons only had to tick over at low revs, with the other tank at the rear in no danger of being outpaced and left behind. Taking double the time to get back and having only encountered sporadic enemy activity, they were forced to close down as the weather began to darken and the wind picked up to blow a stinging rain into their faces. That rain and wind made clear promises to bring more and far worse with it, and just as the weather brought them misery, they found their way blocked by a knot of shambling Screechers heading away from them. Hearing the engines, the group stopped and rotated to face the new source of sound that sparked their interest. They could smell no flesh, and simply stared at the stationary tank to see if it became edible.

From the centre of the group, one of the creatures stepped out to push its way through the cluster of dead. They had all encountered the faster ones, the fresher ones, but none of them had seen one that was so small yet. The girl must have been no older than eight, her plaited hair swaying as she tilted her blood-soaked face to regard the hulks of metal. She took two tentative steps forwards, far more controlled and coordinated than the others clustered around her, and she peered hard at the forward hull.

Inside the tank, Captain Palmer took his eyes away from the goggles providing his view ahead and rubbed them.

"Wells," he said tiredly, apologetically, "drive on, please."

Wells sighed, selected a forward gear, and eased the tracks over the group to flatten them all in a rolling, crunching, hissing mess that left their hearts heavy.

Reaching a junction in the road that was the demarcation line between heading west and them needing to turn directly south, Sergeant Horton in the rear-most tank swore loudly over the radio, before following up with a rushed report.

"Enemy rear, fucking thousands of them, go, go!"

As they were already moving at close to their top speed, firing themselves up to move faster was something of a pointless exercise.

Strauss tried again and again to raise anyone on the radio, but something in the rapidly worsening atmospherics was garbling his transmission.

~

Peter ran.

He clearly saw the direction of the herd trampling their way over the landscape, so he turned a right angle away from that line and he bolted across country to escape. He ran into the gathering storm and darkening skies to cross fences and duck under hedges, until he was so exhausted that he dropped to the wet dirt and stayed there, letting the rain just fall on him.

He hadn't uttered a sound since the gasp back at the farm, and still kept his mouth firmly closed. He was lost, but that didn't bother him. Being lost only mattered when you had somewhere to be, somewhere to get back to, but seeing as he no longer had a home, the concept of not knowing where he was seemed like an irrelevance that held no feelings of fear for him.

Home was a theory. Something from the past that didn't feature in the present, but which might do one day in his future. Getting to his feet, his face a rictus of determination and his eyes devoid of emotion, he put one foot in front of the other and carried on.

Arriving at the outskirts of a village, Peter crouched in the hedge, watching and listening as the rain soaked him, until he was sure that nothing was moving before he slipped low towards the first house. He tried the door, marvelling that the first one he went to yielded. He moved the pitchfork out in front of him as he crept into the hallway. Looking down, he saw that the floor was polished wood with the last of the day's light glowing along the length of it, and the warm orange glow made him feel somehow safer. Standing tall and sucking in a deep breath through his nose, he rapped the handle of his pitchfork loudly on the wooden floor four times and waited.

He counted off the seconds in his head, waiting for the hissing and the moaning to start that would tell him how many were there and where they were. Nothing answered his loud taps, so he repeated them with even more volume than before.

Still nothing answered, so he slowly walked through the small house and checked the rooms one by one. Returning to the front door he slid over the heavy bolt and checked that the back door was similarly secure, before he slipped the bag off his shoulders and went to the bathroom, where he stripped his soaking wet, shit-caked and filthy clothes and ran a sink of cold water to clean himself with a flannel and a bar of soap.

Using the soft, white towel rested over the radiator he dried himself and stopped, trying to figure out when he had stopped hating being cold.

He stood shivering, naked and barely clean, and realised that something so simple as just being cold no longer mattered to him. It was as though that part of him, the scared child he had been, was gone. Relishing being cold and feeling his skin tighten with the early evening air, he wandered into the bedroom and rested his eyes on the portable cassette player and headphones beside the bed.

The bed wasn't made, and he only then had the impression that he was intruding for the first time. He took the cassette player and returned to the bathroom.

Wrapping the towel around him, he padded back downstairs and emptied out his backpack to find the set of fresh clothes he had thought to pack. He had decided to give up on the set he had been wearing, thinking that their prolonged contact with the various noxious substances was taking viable wearing of them again a stretch too far.

Dressed, he used the kitchen sink to clean his pitchfork before leaving it on the table with the rest of his collection of kit, and then opened the cupboards to take out the things he could eat.

After a cold supper of rice pudding eaten straight from the can, Peter dragged duvets downstairs to make a warm, soft den on the large settee. Before he drifted off to sleep, he listened to the song on the tape over and over, feeling the sadness of the female lyrics and the power of the chorus course through him, and he decided that this was the way forward for him from now on.

With the fuzzy coverings of the flimsy earphones over his head, Peter could hear the thunderous sound of rolling gunfire booming heavily and desperately on the distant coast.

Chapter 24

"Roger," Daniels spoke into the radio, before turning to Johnson and giving a confident thumbs-up. Johnson knew that he was talking to Maxwell's picquet, the armoured screen deployed ahead of their position, and that they had just reported the arrival of their Sabre troop with the resupply wagon and the two main battle tanks.

Johnson allowed himself a small sigh of relief as the constant garbled transmissions had begun to cause him some stress. Raising the binoculars to the tracked vehicle he could see at the very end of the road, he saw the long barrel of the tank's massive gun bob into view and stop next to the Spartan. The tank stopped, then Daniels spoke in response to the radio that had burst to life excitedly.

"Stand by, one," he said, turning to Johnson and wearing a wide-eyed look of fear, "Sir, units report heavy concentration of enemy moving along this road."

Johnson's face stayed resolutely still and expressionless. 'This road' led only one place, and that was directly at him and his men on their very newly-acquired island. Raising the binoculars, he looked directly ahead to the furthest limits of his view.

"Well isn't that just fucking marvellous..." he sighed to himself, prompting Daniels to ask, "Sir?"

"Pull them back," he said looking ahead to the valley with its high ground on each side leading to the sea, "there's nowhere for them to go, so we mount a defence here and set a killing field at the land side of the bridge."

Daniels looked, knowing that a concentration of fire on the roadway would likely ruin the surface and make life difficult, but he decided against offering that opinion, as a heavy concentration of enemy marching up the road to eat them would likely make life even more difficult.

Orders were given, armoured cars moved into position all over the lower parts of the town where they could bring their guns to bear on the approaching horde. Johnson ordered the two Fox wagons out of the roadway and asked, via Daniels on the radio, if their two new additions would oblige him by blocking the road with the higher-profile back ends of their tanks. The request, not an order because a) they weren't his troops and b) they had an officer down there somewhere, was acknowledged.

Only then did the problems truly begin.

The four Foxes and their fuel resupply wagon rolled over the bridge, luckily one sturdy enough to cope with eighty tonnes of tank, otherwise the plan would have had to have been revised, and the tanks pulled aside at the landward edge of the roadway, to allow the Spartans to squeak and trundle their way through the gap.

Only the last one, too far away for Johnson to hear, juddered to an ailed stop a hundred or so paces from the threshold. Daniels bent to his radio, no doubt receiving a transmission that would mean he would update the SSM as soon as he could, but Johnson's nerve broke first.

"Mechanical failure?" he asked the man who was forced to try and listen to two people at once.

"Stand by," he said quickly into the radio, then spoke rapidly to Johnson, "gearbox linkage," he said, "and something else, they can't even roll it out of the way," then turned his attention back to the radio to speak again.

Shit, shit, shit, Johnson thought to himself, wasting precious seconds before turning back, "Tell them to dismount and leave it. Get their arses back over here and ask one of the Chieftains if they can push it aside."

It wasn't that he was precious about the loss of one of their tracked light tanks, not overly anyway, but more that the position it had broken down in directly obscured a large area where the oncoming Screechers would be shielded from fire by the armour. He turned and gave another order for as much of their other guns, the 30mm cannons on the Foxes, to drive higher into the island to see if they could find a place to bring their guns to bear on the approach. Four of them sparked noisily to life and drove out to find some elevation.

"Sir, Sergeant Maxwell is reporting he can fix it," Daniels said to him before adding, "he thinks."

He raised the binoculars, scanning the front to see the horizon darkened by a crowd the size of which he had never seen. Ahead of that crowd, that darkening line comprising, he knew, teeth and relentless malice, he could see individual shapes breaking off and moving faster than the crowd behind. Not much, but faster nonetheless. The limit of his view was, give or take, a mile.

Average walking speed is three miles per hour, he told himself, *one mile in twenty minutes, especially over rough ground, which means half that for the Leaders… and take away twenty percent for me being wrong.*

"Tell him," Johnson said testily to Daniels, "that *I* think he has about eight minutes before he is up to his nutsack in the faster type of bastard Screecher." Daniels nodded and paraphrased the instructions in relay.

"Ask the last Chieftain to advance, hold firm and lay down covering fire," he said to complete his thought, then listened as the request was passed on and he glanced forward without the need to use the binoculars, and watched the tank surge away to push the protection out in front. A few seconds later, the change in sound washed over him as the pulsing revs of the huge engine reached his ears to offer a delayed soundtrack to the emerging show.

"Five minutes," he told Daniels, "then order the Chieftain to withdraw. Maxwell's wagon had better be dismounted and abandoned before then."

Daniels nodded, understanding that he was to give the orders to abandon an asset long before the risk of being overrun became critical. Just as he did so, he flinched and spun his head back to the front to the source of the noise. That clattering noise was the two heavy machine guns on the tank, one coaxial and firing as the big turret moved, and the other operated independently by the commander in his cupola. They were engaging the enemy out in front of the main force, holding their ground and pouring fire and lead towards them.

Johnson couldn't see the tank, but he could hear it. He heard it then, and heard the engines roaring as it came back into view in evident withdrawal.

"Sir, Chieftain is reporting too many enemy to engage," Daniels told him. He nodded at the radio operator, who ordered the tank to fall back and for the crew of the stranded Spartan to abandon their task. Johnson cursed himself then, as nobody had thought to send a vehicle out to them in time so that they now faced a humiliating flight on foot to reach safety. The guns of the tank rattled in the distance as it crept back towards the bridge, where one lane was still open.

"Negative, abandon and rejoin immediately," Daniels said insistently into the radio, then listened and turned to Johnson, wearing an exasperated look as he repeated the order.

"Sir, Maxwell thinks he almost has it," he said to the SSM.

Johnson opened his mouth and drew breath to rage down the radio at the Sergeant he counted as a friend. His anger wasn't through being disobeyed, but was born of fear that he would lose the man to the army of Screechers marching on them. Staying closed down in their wagon was suicide, as even one stray 30mm round could kill them all with a lucky ricochet, let alone the Chieftains firing 120mm rounds that would slice through them with sickening ease, and superheat everything inside their tank as it went.

Just as he went to press the switch to speak, the radio crackled and burst into life.

"Got it!" screamed the excited voice of Maxwell's driver.

Johnson thrust the binoculars up to his face to locate the tracked vehicle and saw two men scrambling to climb down feet first into the hatches as the light tank bucked and crawled towards them with agonisingly slow progress. Johnson guessed that the crew had managed to get the linkage connected to just one gear, and that gear did not afford them a particularly speedy flight, but they were moving, and they should get back just in time. The horde was approaching the front of the tank at a worryingly close distance now, and all over the island, nervous men wiped hands and foreheads as they waited for the order to fire.

"All wagons, degrade the enemy concentration, do not fire at the leading edge until the units are secure..." Johnson paused after giving the order and allowing time for each gunner to switch their aim to the massed section of dead now visible, "...fire when ready."

He didn't get to finish his order, because firing switches were depressed the second they heard the word *fire*. Their immediate universe erupted in a noise far worse than their barrages before, as almost every gun in the squadron opened up at once. Using the binoculars, Johnson could see body parts flying high above the lurching crowd, along with great gouts of earth and other detritus.

No infantry in the history of the world would advance into that kind of fire, he knew, but then infantry, as much as it pained him to accept even then, had brains. No *thinking* enemy would advance into that fire, he corrected himself, and carried on watching as the deepest levels of hell were visited upon the undead.

Then his face dropped, because he realised it wasn't going to be enough.

Even though every gun they had had been brought to bear, the enemy were too many and they had begun to erode their numbers too late to stop them from reaching the makeshift blockage on the bridge. Those two tanks, even with their higher rear ends facing the onslaught instead of the very low-profile fronts, could not hope to remain where they were without being swarmed over, and as soon as the enemy reached their manned armour then the barrage of their sixteen heavier cannons must stop or they risked killing the tank crews and blocking their only road off the island. Anticipating this somehow, the Captain in the tank below called them on their radio.

"Machine guns only when they get to us," he said, "30mm to the main body of the assault only,"

Johnson heard Daniels acknowledge the order, unnecessarily given, then frowned as the Captain spoke again, "If we are overrun, we will advance the tanks into the assault. Stand by to replace the obstruction with light armour imminently," he said.

Daniels looked at Johnson, both men incredulous and admiring of the bravery they had just heard.

The two tank crews, risking becoming stranded and dying of dehydration closed down inside their machines, planned to hold off until the very last moment then drive straight over the oncoming zombies and crush their way through the attack at their own risk. Behind them, the four tracked vehicles of Maxwell's troop, including his own limping wagon, could block the road as though they were standing shoulder to shoulder, and could still use their cupola-mounted machine guns without posing a risk to the tank crews or themselves as they fired.

It was a desperate move, as any surviving attackers could then swarm over the smaller vehicles blocking the road and invade their uninfected haven, but it was all they had left.

"Captain, this is the SSM," Johnson answered on the radio personally, breaking radio code with one their conventional sins of using manes or ranks, "orders understood, Sir, God speed."

With that, just as the leading wave of angry, hungry, undead flesh met the rear of the armour, both tanks reversed in unison and slicked the roadway instantly with gallons of blood from the flattened, destroyed bodies.

The four Spartans pressed up to take their place at the roadblock, and even though the guns all still fired incessantly, they all watched as the two huge tanks drove through the horde, turned, and drove side by side to carve an enormous wave out of the attack, before the bodies swarmed over them to obscure the armour from sight entirely.

Heads dropped, hopes were dashed, and the radio crackled into life once more.

"Tower," said a voice in a bad American accent, "this is Ghost Rider, requesting a fly-by…"

"Last callsign, identify?" Daniels snapped back into the set, annoyed that anyone would break radio protocol with such poorly-timed levity.

The voice came back, no longer attempting the impression, "Cease fire, cease fire," it said, "friendly air assets inbound, acknowledge cease fire order."

Johnson shrugged in disbelief and nodded, then watched as Daniels picked up the squadron radio and ordered everyone to cease fire. Confused or not, they followed the orders.

"Confirmed… Ghost Rider?" Daniels said with a wince into the other set, as he had no other thoughts on what to call the newcomers, "cease fire is confirmed."

No verbal answer came, but the insistent *wop-wop-wop* of rotary wings soon pierced the air now that the gunfire had subsided.

Bursting high from over a cliff, a pair of twin grey-painted Sea King helicopters chattered noisily into their world and impressed them all with a staggering display. From the aft end of the lead helicopter's belly burst flare after flare which spread out in diagonal streaks of fire and smoke, and just as the soldiers on the ground found their attention drawn inexorably towards the show, so too did the head of every last Screecher stop and rotate upwards to watch the bright, noisy thing settle into a hover just three hundred feet above them.

"Cut all engines, apply all safety catches, stub out your smokes, keep your tray-tables in the upright positions and your seats upright," said the voice on the radio which, if the spectacle in front of them hadn't been so incredible, would likely have boiled the top off any NCO for the ill-disciplined approach to radio procedure. Johnson shrugged and nodded again to Daniels, who relayed the order to the squadron.

His words trailed off into a, "fuuuck me!" as his eyes drank in the scene below. The army of undead, the wide swathes of corpses flooding over the landscape to wash over them, now began to bunch together. The crowd started to swell in the centre, then it grew in height as they commenced an unrehearsed circus routine.

They climbed each other, hand over hand, body over body, as they stretched upwards to reach the violently spinning machine. The second helicopter also stayed in a hover, only another few hundred feet above and to the side of the first, the pilot of which was using it as the world's most elaborate and expensive lure.

Just as the show couldn't get any stranger, Johnson heard the distant but distinct sound of a familiar guitar riff blasting out over the open air of their small valley. Snatching up the binoculars, he managed to catch a glimpse of the open side door on the lower bird and what he saw made his mouth drop open and echo the recent sentiment Daniels had made.

"Fuck me," he said in a small squeak of a voice, before adding his customary, "Christ on a bloody bike."

His eyes had registered a huge speaker, like the kind one would see adorning the stage of a huge rock concert, which was secured to the helicopter's deck with bright straps. That wasn't what had prompted the blasphemy, however, that was reserved for the realisation of what song was being played over it.

That familiar guitar sound, that fast, frantic and intense beat, and the unmistakable tone of the vocals coursed through him and forced a smile to his bewildered face as he automatically mouthed along with the lyrics that he knew.

The song stopped, and after a brief pause of twenty seconds it began again, filling the rural coastline with *Ace Of Spades*, which led the desperate and feverish crowd of zombies up the slopes of the steep hill as the helicopters led them away like some awful, grotesque pied-piper. Nobody said a word as the leading edge of the remaining zombie horde reached the edge of the cliff where they could see the man in the open side door.

Johnson couldn't see him, but he was playing air guitar with enough gusto that the approaching Screechers cried out in an attempt to drown out the music and reach for him, only between them and him was thirty feet of open air and a three-hundred-and-forty-foot drop to the rocks and sea below. They came to him like lemmings, throwing themselves off the cliff unthinkingly in their pathological need for flesh. The song stopped and was rewound, then the air guitar solo began again. It was repeated three more times until the last of the shuffling, awkward corpses made their final journey courtesy of gravity.

The helicopters drew back from the cliff, flying sedately towards the top of the island, and the radio crackled again.

"Tower," it said in the same awful accent as before, "this is Ghost Rider, requesting fly-by…"

Daniels looked at Johnson expectantly, who shrugged at him one more time as though the world had just become so strange that even he didn't know what to say.

Turning back to the radio set, Daniels smiled ruefully at Johnson as though asking permission and responded in an equally poor accent, "Negative, Ghost Rider, the pattern is full…"

The responding hail was full of laughter and cheering, and deservedly so, because the two Sea Kings of the Commando Helicopter Force had just saved the cavalry.

Epilogue

The helicopters landed, and the crews and passengers were brought down the hill of the island by Bedford truck to the command centre adopted on a whim by Johnson. Being pilots, all of them were officers, but the few crew members including the air guitarist, were non-commissioned ranks. The second helicopter, the one that stayed up and away from the main danger, held a belly full of Royal Marines under the leadership of a Lieutenant and a Sergeant.

The tanks' crews, uncovered from their burial under dead flesh by the unorthodox actions of the Naval pilots and crew, had returned to the bridge, their vehicles were in a disgusting state and would need significant clearing, as entire limbs and torsos were caught in the running gear. But their eight men came out unscathed. The look of shock and child-like relief on Second Lieutenant Palmer's face was almost embarrassing for the men close enough to witness the reunion of older and younger brother, and Captain Palmer's effusive greeting to Squadron Sergeant Major Johnson was full of praise and admiration for the unit, the men, and the leadership displayed under the terrible circumstances. He had the good grace and manners not to mention that the squadron did well despite not having leadership, but Johnson was beginning to reckon that Palmer senior was nothing like Palmer junior, and that he rated men on merit.

From what he had heard already, the man was competent and switched-on, and reports from Strauss and the tank crews had all reinforced the reputation surrounding him as positive. With that in mind, Johnson asked the Captain for a word in private.

The two men stepped into a doorway and saw that Lieutenant Palmer made to follow them, but his older brother held up a subtle hand, which was accepted without malice. Seeing how easily he handled the brash young man impressed Johnson, which made it easier to say what he needed to say next.

"Sir, now that you're here I should relinquish command of the squadron to you," he said formally, expecting the effusive praise to continue and for his insistence that the Captain needed some recovery time and that the SSM should continue in his adopted role of commander.

"You have my thanks, Mister Johnson," Captain Palmer said, "both personally for keeping Olly in one piece and as a soldier for a job bloody well done," Johnson smiled, anticipating his imminent field promotion, "I shall require a full disposition list to include staffing, both rostered, and whatever temporary promotions you may have had to make, as well as our supply situation and ammunition count," Palmer said, sparking straight back into business.

Johnson blinked, thrown straight back down the leadership ladder in a split-second.

"I highly doubt our presence here will remain a secret to the enemy, even though we've likely cleared out most of the... what did you call them... the Screechers... in the county with that last little skirmish," Palmer said. "I'll address the men by troop tonight, no point in having a parade just to introduce the new *Rupert*, eh?" he smiled self-effacingly and continued, "now, shall we bring in the Navy chaps?"

Johnson nodded numbly, opening the door to invite the men inside.

Introductions took a couple of minutes, even though the invitation was extended only to the four pilots and the Marine Lieutenant.

"As far as we know," Lieutenant Commander John Barrett announced, "the entire UK has been affected by the outbreak and only the odd pocket of resistance has remained... human, shall we say," he scanned the eyes in the room to see that he hadn't lost anyone yet, "Yeovilton was abandoned late this afternoon as it was deemed, 'indefensible' by the Royal Marines," the young marine officer nodded his agreement, no doubt recalling the miles and miles of perimeter fence in need of guarding, "and air assets have been dished out where they are needed most."

"The Invincible is in the channel," said the other helicopter pilot as he glibly gave the news of an aircraft carrier floating not far away. He was the same rank as Barrett. This pilot had introduced himself as Murray but answered his fellow pilots when they called him Ruby.

He continued, "and command have doled out the birds all over the place. We have a small detachment on their way by road, carrying a tanker of fuel for our aircraft, and protected by the Marines."

Johnson nodded at him, conveying that the necessary requirements to meet and accommodate that convoy would be made.

"Military bases are still active in Scotland," said Barrett, but as of yet, we have no assets on the south coast except your Squadron, so here we are," he finished with a smile.

"What about Germany?" Captain Palmer asked quietly. Johnson kicked himself mentally then, recalling that Palmer was on leave from his own squadron based near Berlin.

Barrett and Murray exchanged a look before Murray answered, "Gone. And our active units over the water," meaning the thousands of personnel deployed to the conflict in Northern Ireland and beyond, "are reporting outbreaks of their own."

"So," Barrett said with a clap of his hands and forced joviality, "we are to consolidate and rescue as many of the civilian population as possible whilst Her Majesty's government decides what to do."

"What about the swarming behaviour of the Screechers?" Johnson asked. Smirks rippled around the pilots at his mention of the nickname, flashing anger behind the SSM's eyes as Barrett laughed at him overtly.

———

"Have you been face-to-face with one yet, Sir?" he asked gently. Despite the low tone that he had been careful to sanitise for any trace of hostility, the air in the room dropped a clear five degrees.

"No, Sergeant Major," he responded carefully, "I have not. Instead I fly the better part of ten tonnes of helicopter and am responsible for the lives of my crew and passengers. So, no, Sergeant Major, I haven't been face-to-face with one, yet."

Barrett's over-reaction to the question showed his embarrassment almost instantly, and he dialled back the hostility immediately and turned to Murray. The two seemed to be deliberating using only their eyebrows until Murray shrugged and turned to the soldiers.

"They exhibit a kind of herding behaviour, and tend to amass around individual infected subjects, sorry - *Screechers* – in groups of roughly one hundred. Three times, that we know of, there have been mass clusterings in as many days. Two of them dissipated. The other, well," he shrugged with a smirk, "the other ended up taking the long drop."

"The other two swarms dissipated by themselves?" Captain Palmer asked intently.

"Indeed," Barrett said, "it seems they are drawn by sound," he explained, as though the soldiers hadn't been able to figure that fact out yet, "and unless something really loud attracts their attention, the noise they make together sort of makes them lose interest and they wander off from the fringes."

"How do you know this?" Johnson asked, seeing the familiar exchange of looks as though he was asking for the combination to a safe.

"The Americans have AWACS over us as of this morning," he admitted reluctantly.

"So," Palmer interjected politely, "our colonial cousins are able to spy on us from a safe thirty-thousand feet but not offer any assistance?"

"Captain," Barrett said, "it isn't just the Americans… It's all of NATO, or at least those who are still intact and not fighting their own war. They suspect either a direct Russian attack or at least the threat of nuclear bombardment. Europe is falling to this disease and the Americans have to stop it spreading across the Atlantic. We would do the same."

They would, Palmer thought as he glanced to Johnson and conveyed just how unhappy he was when politics was added to the already toxic mix they swam in.

They bloody would.

~

Peter, the sole of one shoe still flapping loudly on the roadway, slowed his run as he had not heard any of the faster ones and reckoned he had run far enough away to stop and think, without the slower ones catching him up. It had been a mistake, he knew, and not a mistake that he would make again, because he did not wait long enough to watch the houses for signs of movement.

One of the faster ones, in some bizarre approximation of corpse popularity, had gone into the bungalow opposite and the crowd with it had followed. As soon as he had made a noise breaking into the house, they had screeched and lumbered towards him. He had no idea where the faster one was, but he hoped it was stuck inside the house by its own followers being clumsy and blocking the doors.

Having annoyed himself at expending energy without finding food or a warm, dry place to spend the night, he looked around for anywhere to hole up in relative safety.

His luck, he thought with a wry smile of relief, was going to run out soon if he didn't stop making these mistakes that offered such valuable learning opportunities.

Turning at a right angle to the direction he had come from, he took the next small road to his left and walked straight down the middle. In the old world, walking down the middle of the road was tempting fate and would likely get a young boy killed, but in this new world, walking between low walls and stationary cars where dormant corpses could spark to life and bite him was a far bigger risk than being run over by a car.

Nothing jumped out on him, even though he was ready with his pitchfork, and nothing drove down the road, which might have actually been a good thing, so long as it didn't run him over.

He found a detached cottage on the edge of the village he had wandered into, with a neat thatch roof which hung down low over the front door. Peter watched and waited, listening and smelling the air like one of the things he was trying to avoid, and when he was sure it was safe, he waited some more. Eventually deciding to open the door and rap the handle of his pitchfork on the cobbled path, he waited, but nothing came lurching and groaning from the house straight away. Creeping inside, he repeated his process of searching the house, then locking himself in to take what he wanted.

His luck struck again, and he found the room of a boy about his own age, judging by the size of the clothes. He ate, changed and restocked his backpack before settling down to listen to the same song on the tape in his new cassette player. He didn't know who the singer was, but he smiled at the coincidence of the song's lyrics and the small pot of green army figures on the shelf. He took them down, looking at each one in turn as he organised them as per their poses.

The crawling rifleman.

The soldier throwing a grenade.

The kneeling man aiming his long gun.

The officer standing and pointing his pistol.

He mimed along with the words, learned as the routine had established itself in his mind to listen to the song as he settled down in a new home for the night. He lined them all up, then used his finger to poke them and make them topple.

"…like toy soldiers…" he sang softly in time with the music.

END OF BOOK 1, the adventure continues in

Toy Soldiers 2: Aftermath

Don't forget to follow me on Facebook, Twitter and Instagram, and sign up for my newsletter at www.devoncford.com.

Like the book? Leave a review!

DCF

22487517R00168

Made in the USA
San Bernardino, CA
13 January 2019